ONDINE'S CURSE

ONDINE'S CURSE

ANTONIA RACHEL WARD

Ondine's Curse

First published in Great Britain 2025 by Ghost Orchid Press

ISBN (paperback): 978-1-0685207-7-8

ISBN (e-book): 978-1-0685207-6-1

"Dear, you should not stay so late,
Twilight is not good for maidens;
Should not loiter in the glen
In the haunts of goblin men."

— CHRISTINA ROSSETTI,
GOBLIN MARKET

1

———

"And as the evening wanes to night,
And the Moon Lake's tide recedes,
The water nymph comes
'Neath silver light,
To punish man's cruel deeds."

I paused in my recitation to an audience of none, my eye caught by the illustration alongside the lines. The delicate watercolour depicted a nymph lounging on a boulder at the edge of a lake. Her long, silvery hair curled around her shoulders, while the hem of her white dress dipped in the water. There was a wistfulness about her expression that made me sad to look at her. A sigh lingered in her painted blue eyes.

Sitting on my own rock, I emulated the pose, holding the tattered book open with one hand, my bare toes dangling in the little brook that flowed beneath me. Curling my legs to one side, I turned to gaze over my shoulder just as the nymph did in the picture—and spotted my sister crossing the lawn towards me.

Charlotte, who was with child and beginning to show, had an irritating habit of rubbing her swelling belly when she thought no one was looking. Catching herself, she darted her hand behind her back, though not without a fleeting, smug smile.

"Emma! Whatever are you doing with your feet in the water?" Charlotte's eyes widened in horror, and I followed her gaze to see the bottom of my dress dragging in the stream.

"I was only reading."

She sighed. "It's getting late. Edgar will be here soon. And now you're going to have to change." She glanced at my book. "Please don't tell me you're reading that dreadful Lord Vairnruth again."

"It's my favourite poem." I detested how petulant I sounded, like a stubborn child. Yet my sister would insist on treating me as such, as if I weren't nineteen years old and as much a grown woman as she was.

"He's a bad influence." Charlotte struck out back across the lawn, forcing me to hurry after her.

"Why?"

"The *why* is not for you to know. All that matters is that Papa doesn't want you filling your head with Lord Vairnruth's ideas."

"It's a *poem*," I protested. "About a water nymph. There are no *ideas*."

My sister shot me a sly, sidelong glance. "Only because you're too young to understand. Once you're married, you will—"

"Oh, pray don't start with the 'once you're married' nonsense again. You've been married less than a year. What gives you the right to act so superior?"

"I'm only saying that once you're married, you'll see some things differently."

Charlotte's hand drifted to her belly once more, and I bristled. Ever since her marriage, she'd dropped hints about some secret knowledge she'd gained upon her wedding night. The worst of it: I *was* curious to know what happened between man and wife. Dreadfully so. Charlotte had told me enough to pique my interest, but no more, and at times it was all I could think about. But I was a maiden still, and all I could do was read my books—poetry, novels, romance—and imagine what secrets lay unspoken between the lines.

I rolled my eyes at my sister's complacent expression, but by then we'd reached the driveway, and my sarcastic retort was whipped from my lips when I put my bare foot down on sharp gravel.

"Ouch!"

Charlotte looked down. "Where are your shoes?"

"I ... must have left them by the stream."

"*Emma.*"

"I'll fetch them. It will only take a moment. You go inside."

Sighing, Charlotte turned and waddled towards the front door. I hitched up my skirts and ran back across the grass. The wind hit my face, cool and fresh, making me feel as light as feather, and I laughed with the simple delight of it as I swept up my shoes and sped back. Pausing at the edge of the driveway, I slipped them on and crunched across the gravel, before heading into the entrance hall.

Crawford Manor was a modest home as country piles went. Only half-a-dozen bedrooms, plus space for the servants, of course. The hall's white-tiled floor was buffed to a shine, and a sprig of fresh wildflowers adorned a vase by the door. Charlotte, too, looked pristine, waiting by the stairs in her pink gown, her light brown hair neatly curled and pinned.

The only blot on the unsullied landscape was me—I looked down to see a muddy puddle forming around my feet, thanks to my sodden dress.

Charlotte tutted. "Go up and get changed. I'll send Sarah to help you. Wear something nice. The blue silk dress, perhaps. And *please* re-pin your hair. You look as though you've been through a hedge backwards."

Older sisters. With a huff, I headed upstairs and shut myself in my room, closing the door a little harder than was strictly necessary. While I waited for the maid to appear, I wandered to the window, still holding my book. The volume I'd been reading when my sister so rudely interrupted me was my much-beloved copy of *The Water Nymph* by Lord Augustus Vairnruth, undoubtedly the most famous—and certainly the most talented—poet in all of England. Perhaps all the world. His tragic tale of an innocent maiden cursed by a jealous Faerie King had bewitched my imagination, and since I first discovered it, not a day had gone by that I hadn't found the time to sink myself into the poem's enchanting depths. The lyrical verse, the exotic setting, the exquisite romance ... all had captivated me until I was quite unable to think of anything else. Certainly not tedious dinners with my family. *Certainly* not our esteemed guest, Edgar Goodwin.

There was a timid knock on the door, and Sarah crept inside. She bobbed a small curtsey before opening my wardrobe.

"Lady Melrose says you're to wear the blue silk, if it please you, miss." she said, relaying my sister's command. I had half a mind to argue, but recognising that it was Charlotte who riled me, not the maid, I checked myself and only nodded. Though it pained me to admit it, Sarah was the closest thing to a friend I had in Crawford Manor.

"You'll be dining with Mr Goodwin tonight, I suppose?"

Sarah ventured, as she took my gown from the wardrobe. "You'll want to look your best."

"I want to look presentable. As always."

"Naturally, miss."

Once my dress was laced up and she was re-pinning my hair, Sarah said, "Is Mr Goodwin very handsome, then, miss?"

"Handsome? I can't say I've ever noticed whether or not he is handsome. Perhaps he might be considered so, but what interest would it be of mine?"

"What indeed, ma'am?" Sarah stepped back to examine my hair. "Perhaps a little something else ... These!" She plucked some fresh cornflowers from a vase on my dressing table and arranged them in my hair. "See? They bring out your eyes."

I turned to the looking glass. She was right—the blue of the cornflowers did indeed match my eyes, and they stood out strikingly against my dark hair, too.

"How pretty you look, ma'am," she said. Then, slyly, "I'm sure Mr Goodwin will think so, too."

With a sudden flush of anger, I pulled the cornflowers from my hair and tossed them on the dressing table. "I wish I could tell Mr Goodwin I don't care what he thinks."

Turning away from the looking glass, I walked out, feeling guilty for taking out my anger on the maid. I knew what was really bothering me, just as I knew the reason behind Sarah's sly looks, and my sister's insistence that I wear my finest dress. My parents hadn't spoken to me about it, not directly, but Mr Goodwin had been at the house increasingly often, and a terrible suspicion was growing in the pit of my stomach—a suspicion that hardened into certitude by the time I reached the bottom of the stairs and stood hesitating in front of the drawing room door.

Mr Goodwin was going to propose tonight. And my parents were expecting me to say yes.

2

I steeled myself, trying to settle my fluttering nerves. Me? Marry Mr Goodwin? How had I not seen it before? All those dinner parties and quiet afternoon teas my parents had invited him to. The walks and picnics we'd taken alongside Charlotte and her husband. How could I have been so foolish not to have suspected what they had in mind?

But of course, I *had* suspected. I simply hadn't wanted to admit it. I'd wanted to stay in my own little world with Lord Vairnruth and the water nymph for as long as I could. And now I was going to reap the consequences of my self-imposed ignorance: I had no idea how to act, or what to say. I had done nothing whatsoever to put Mr Goodwin off, and it was possible that I had even inadvertently led him to believe I might say yes.

But I was getting ahead of myself. Perhaps, I thought desperately, I was reading the situation all wrong. Perhaps he was not here to propose at all. With a shaking hand, I pushed open the door.

In the drawing room, Charlotte sat with her feet on a footstool, trying to cool herself with a painted fan while her husband, Francis—a man of stork-like proportions with a nose that greatly resembled a beak—fussed over her. It was a warm evening, and in her delicate condition, my sister felt the heat greatly. Beside them, my mother expounded at great length about which scullery maid Charlotte ought to choose to replace a girl who had recently gotten herself with child: "There are three girls in the village who might suit, but of those I would recommend only two. The other is known for her loose ways. I should not have her under my roof, if I were you. Not unless you want a repeat of last time ..."

Meanwhile, my father stood by the fireplace, talking with Edgar Goodwin. They turned to me when I entered, and my father gave me an appraising look.

"I'm so glad you've decided to grace us with your presence, Emma."

I cast my eyes down and bobbed a small curtsey. "Good evening, father. Good evening, Mr Goodwin."

"Good evening, Miss Crawford." Mr Goodwin took my hand and kissed it. "May I take this opportunity to tell you how delightful you look tonight."

No, you may not, I thought, but I suppose he took my look of embarrassment as proof that his advances were welcome, because his face lit up with a smile.

With his sandy blond hair, light eyes, and clear skin, Mr Goodwin was as handsome as Sarah could have hoped. He led me through to the dining room and we took our seats side by side. I glanced at him out of the corner of my eye. At nearly thirty, he was ten years older than me, and had a decent living as the parish rector. He was not a bad match for a younger daughter with a very meagre dowry, and I knew I was not as pretty as Charlotte. Her full figure and rosy cheeks had managed to catch the eye of a baronet. I, skinny with ebony-dark hair and a pale complexion, was not likely to be so lucky.

And yet, and yet ... As I tried to calmly sip my wine, a mad desperation seized me, as though I were being walked to the gallows. I couldn't quite articulate, even to myself, why I had such a strong aversion to the idea of marrying Edgar Goodwin, yet I knew in the depths of my heart that I could not. I was not ready. I thought I had more time. I had imagined balls and parties, trips to London and Bath. All the new people I might meet, the friends I would make.

I had imagined a lover, someone like the Faerie King who seduced the water nymph when she was still a human maiden named Ondine. A man of sublime beauty, with hair like spun gold and eyes like stars, who would be so overcome with passion for me that he would offer me eternal life if only I would return to his magical land with him. And if I could not have all that, I thought, I would settle for someone who made my stomach flutter with butterflies when I looked at him. Someone with a mind like my own, with whom I could share ideas and dreams as equals. A soulmate, I suppose.

None of that would happen if I were wife to a rector, living out the rest of my days in a small cottage in the next village. I felt the world shrink around me like a vice.

"Are you quite well, Miss Crawford?"

I plastered on a smile. "Very well, thank you, Mr Goodwin."

"Please, call me Edgar. We have known each other long enough by now, I am sure." He began carving his steak into neat cubes. "Your sister tells me you spent the afternoon reading. I'm very fond of reading myself."

"Indeed?" I looked at Charlotte, hoping she would extricate me from this conversation, but she refused to meet my eye.

"Do you have a favourite author?" Edgar went on.

"Lord Vairnruth," I answered without thinking, my enthusiasm bubbling up in spite of my wish to appear cool and noncommittal. "His poems are simply heavenly."

"Vairnruth!" Edgar's eyebrows shot up, and I knew right away that I had made an error. No doubt he was thinking, as my sister did, of Lord Vairnruth's controversial reputation. *Good. The less he likes me, the better.*

"My sister's taste is still developing," said Charlotte, solemnly. "What books would you recommend to her, Edgar?"

"Books? Well, I'm sure Miss Crawford is already well acquainted with Fordyce's *Sermons to Young Women ...*"

"Very well acquainted," I answered, trying to hide the sour expression that threatened to creep onto my face at the thought of that hectoring tome. "But I much prefer novels. Mrs Radcliffe, for example, is a favourite of mine."

"The trouble with novels, Emma," my father cut in, "is that they fill your head with unrealistic ideas." There was a warning edge to his voice. He turned to Edgar. "Sometimes my daughter forgets that she lives in nineteenth-century England, not a fairy tale. But a little careful guidance would soon cure her of such fancies."

I shuddered inwardly. I didn't want to be *cured* of anything. But I kept my face passive, smiling politely as my father launched into his oft-repeated rant against novels. His argument, which he had made to me many times, amounted to the idea that women did not require—indeed, should not *have*—an inner world of any kind. Women, as far as my father would have it, were supposed to look beautiful, behave impeccably, and have heads as empty as dressmaker's mannequins.

"Vairnruth was an old schoolfellow of mine," Edgar said cheerfully. "We were at Cambridge together."

I looked at him anew.

"Is that so?" Francis said. "Were you acquainted with him?"

"Very well acquainted. We ran with the same crowd. We were good friends, in fact."

A surprised silence settled over the table. That a rector could have been friends with Lord Vairnruth was an impossible idea to reconcile. Everyone had heard the rumours about Vairnruth: his many affairs, his wild exploits—several of which had happened at university, just at the time Edgar claimed to have known him. And he was a genius—a man of unrivalled literary talent and imagination. Whereas Edgar was just ... Edgar. I had never heard an interesting word drop from his lips in all the weeks I'd known him.

"In fact," Edgar glanced sidelong at me, "he has invited me to his birthday celebrations next week. His house is not far from here, you know. Just a day's journey or so, in the heart of Derbyshire."

I said nothing. I felt like a fish on a hook, being lured in. Yet my heart fluttered as I imagined the birthday celebrations his Lordship might have. Surely something decadent and fabulous. Perhaps Edgar was not as boring as I had assumed.

"How fascinating," said Francis. "You will have to tell us all about it."

"Mr Goodwin will not be going, I am sure," said my father.

"On the contrary," said Edgar. "I wouldn't miss it for the world."

My mouth twitched at the sight of my father's astonished expression, and Edgar shot me a look as if to say, 'See, we might have fun together after all.'

Soon after, the conversation moved on to Francis and Charlotte's plans to modernise their home, and I finished my dinner in silence. I had nothing to add to the discussion of house extensions and garden renovations. Such things had never interested me, and soon my attention drifted. I began to daydream about Lord Vairnruth's birthday celebrations. What might his house be like? What kind of ball would he throw? It would surely be extravagant and beautiful, like stepping into a wonderland. I doubted anything my imagination could conjure up would come close to the truth of it, but that did not stop me from trying. If only there were some way I could find out for myself.

After dinner, we retreated to the drawing room, and before long Edgar approached me.

"Miss Crawford," he said, smiling. "You must be hot here beside the fire. Perhaps you might join me by the window, where it is cooler?"

I opened my mouth to refuse, then caught my father's eye. I could see he desired me to go, so I rose and followed Edgar to the open window. It *was* cooler there, and the fresh evening air made me shiver as we stood looking out onto the dark lawn. Half hidden by the curtain, he turned to me.

"Miss Crawford, I hope you'll forgive me for orchestrating this opportunity to speak with you privately ..."

"Pray!" I cut in. "Don't say another word, Mr Goodwin, please."

"Your shyness is understandable. And natural, in a young lady such as yourself. But I must assure you that I have your father's blessing. There can be nothing untoward in us conversing together like this—not if, as I fervently hope, we might soon be ... be married." He said this last in a rush, stumbling over his words. "Miss Crawford, would you do me the very great honour of ..."

But I heard no more. Blood rushed to my head, the ringing in my ears blocking out all other sound. I turned from Edgar and hurried out of the room, only stopping when I reached the hallway and had the space to breathe once more. I raised my trembling hands to my face and screamed silently. When I turned around, I found my father behind me.

"Emma, what sort of a display do you think you are making?"

"Papa, please." I ran to him and took his hands. "I can't marry Mr Goodwin. I cannot!"

He looked down at me with a frown that made me feel like a naughty child, caught with her hand in the butter churn.

"Mr Goodwin is a better match than you ought to be able to hope for with your dowry," he told me. "You know we can't manage much. Don't throw this opportunity away out of some silly, heedless fancy that you can do better. Who else do you suppose will marry you?"

I pulled my hands from his grasp. "I don't want to marry *anyone*. Not now. Not yet."

Turning away, I ran to the big oak front door and flung it open, hurrying out into the night. I had no idea where I was going—only that I had to get away. Away from Mr Goodwin, from my father, from Charlotte and her smug looks. I ran down the lawn, my way lit only by the lights from the manor and the full moon, and before long I found myself back at the brook, near the rock where I'd been sitting earlier in the day. On a whim, I slipped off my shoes and waded into the water. The cool liquid flowing around my toes calmed me, and I stood there for a long while, dreaming of the Faerie King.

In my mind's eye, he watched me from across the stream, his golden eyes aglow with longing, and *I*—not just mere Emma now, but a beautiful, tantalising nymph—was the object of his desire. He wanted me, only me, with a hunger that drove all else from his mind. I imagined him crossing the water towards me, his gaze fixed on mine. I imagined him running a finger down my cheek and bending down to kiss me —a long, deep kiss that left my body aflame. What would it be like to be kissed so, I wondered? What would he whisper to me? Would he clasp me to him and swear his undying love?

I could almost hear the words. I thought of him pressing his body against mine, his chest against my chest. His hands encircling my waist—

A footstep interrupted my reverie, and I whirled around.

3

*I*t was Edgar. I looked away, trying to compose myself. How had I let my mind run away with me so?

"Miss Crawford," he began, in his formal, stilted way. "I'm sorry to have caused you such distress."

Frustration boiled in me. "If you don't wish to cause me any more, then perhaps you might leave me alone."

"I have no wish to make you miserable," he said. "But I believe there's something I can offer in return for your hand. Something I suspect might make you very happy indeed."

His voice was gentle, and it eased my panic. I looked over my shoulder at him.

"Is that so?"

"If we were engaged, I believe I could persuade your father to let us take a trip together. I imagine you have never spent much time away from this house?"

I nodded. It was true. Apart from a couple of summers spent at my aunt's house near Portsmouth, and an entertaining few weeks in London, I had never been anywhere my whole life.

"And where would you suggest we go?"

"Accompany me to Lord Vairnruth's birthday ball next week."

A lightning bolt of delight shot through me, followed by a feeling of deep despair. "My father would never allow it. And besides, I am not invited."

"Your father wishes to please me, as a potential son-in-law. I believe he will agree to a group outing—your sister and Lord Melrose can accompany us. And as to being invited—his Lordship is an old friend. He will do me this favour, I am sure. I shall write to him tomorrow, and make sure that he has room for us all to stay." He bowed slightly. "It would be an honour to have you accompany me as my wife to be, Miss Crawford."

The thought of visiting Lord Vairnruth's home thrilled me, yet I could not help but ruminate on what I might be giving up if I became Edgar's wife. He seemed a kind man, it was true, and as Sarah had so rightly pointed out, he was not unattractive. And yet I did not love him, and nor did I believe he loved me.

He saw my hesitation, and his face crumpled with disappointment.

"Please, Miss Crawford," he said, his tone changing to one of earnest distress. "I need you. It is vital that you accompany me on this visit, and you know that your father will never allow it unless we are engaged."

I stared at him. "Vital? Why?"

Edgar's cheeks reddened. "It's ... hard to explain. I long to see my old friend, but I can't face him without you by my side. Would you? Please?"

He looked so shy and distressed I almost felt sorry for him. But his request perplexed me. I could not fathom why he would ask such a thing, nor what the consequences might be for me.

"Miss Crawford." Edgar stopped close to me. "I hope you

will consider my proposal, as ... as a friend. It would be an honour to introduce you to your idol, and for my part, I would be most grateful for your support."

There was an earnestness in his eyes that made me feel that there was something more in his desire to see his friend—something I could not quite begin to understand.

"You really need me?" I said.

Edgar nodded. "Miss Crawford ..."

"Emma, please."

"Emma. How can I explain this? I've always been the sort of man who would never marry. A confirmed bachelor, you understand?"

I wasn't entirely sure I did, but I waited for him to go on, and so he continued:

"At Cambridge, there were rumours about me. About my ... predilections. Many shunned me. Lord Vairnruth did not. He has no fear of scandal—indeed, he embraces it. But that makes him a dangerous man for someone in my position. If I were to attend his ball alone, with all our old university fellows there, I should be inviting the kind of accusations upon myself that would risk my expulsion from the Church, the end of my career. Perhaps even jail." He grimaced. "For these reasons I have avoided visiting his Lordship for several years. If I attended with a fiancée, I would appear respectable. I could deflect the rumours. *That* is why I need you. I tell you this, Emma, because I see something in you. A kindred spirit perhaps. I trust you to understand, and not to hate me for what I am."

As he spoke, I began to put two and two together, and felt a rush of pity for him. And yet, honest as he had been, it didn't change the fact that my father was expecting me to marry him. What would my life look like, wedded to a man who had considered himself a 'confirmed bachelor'? Whose greatest priority was to use me as a respectable cover while he spent time with someone clearly far more important to him? Could he ever come close to the soulmate I had dreamed about? That, surely, was impossible.

These thoughts weighed on my mind as I bade Edgar goodnight. I went upstairs, where Sarah waited in my room. I must have seemed pensive as she helped me undress, for she said shyly that she hoped I'd had a pleasant evening.

"Very pleasant," I replied, without enthusiasm.

"And Mr Goodwin? Did he ...?" Sarah trailed off, no doubt aware that she was overstepping her bounds. But rather than reprimand her, I sighed and sat on the bed, wrapping my dressing gown tight around my shoulders.

"He asked me to marry him, yes." I patted the bed. "Sit with me."

Sarah looked surprised, but sat down all the same. "I hope you don't mind my saying so, miss, but you don't look right happy about it."

"Would you be?" I asked her, genuinely curious.

"Me? I should think so, miss! I can only imagine the fine things I'd have if I were the wife of someone like Mr Goodwin. But I am not you, and you have been brought up to better expectations than me."

"Are fine things all there is to life? I would sooner be poor and free to do as I pleased, I think."

Sarah smiled slightly. "Forgive me, miss, but I should think that's easier to say when you've never been poor."

"And what about love, Sarah? He doesn't love me, nor I him."

"Many married people are not in love," said Sarah. "But they are happy, and comfortable, don't you think?"

"The arrangement Mr Goodwin has suggested ..." I took a deep breath. "I do not think he would be unkind. I do not think he would trouble me much at all, to tell the truth. And if I go with him, he will take me to Lord Vairnruth's ball. Perhaps he will take me to London, too, or even further afield. I might have a better life with him than I had imagined."

I looked at Sarah, but she only shook her head. "I can't advise you, miss. If it were me, I think I would marry him, but as to yourself, only you can choose."

"You're right, of course." I patted her hand. "Thank you, Sarah. You may go now."

The little maid hurried out, looking relieved, and I lay down in my bed. Now finally alone, I couldn't help returning to the fantasy about the Faerie King I had indulged earlier, and I drifted away into delicious dreams.

EDGAR ARRIVED at the crack of dawn. I found him waiting with my father in the breakfast room. My father got up as I entered, leaving us alone.

I took a seat at the table, but Edgar paced the room restlessly, twisting a napkin in his hands until I thought he would tear it in two.

"I have made a decision," I told him, keen to put him out of his misery as soon as possible. He did not reply, merely nodded at me to go on. His nerves and paleness, I could have attributed to him being sick for love of me, yet I knew better. It was all for Lord Vairnruth, and my wonder that someone could inspire such devotion made me even more curious to meet the man himself. "I will marry you. And if my father permits it, I will go with you to Lord Vairnruth's party."

Edgar let out an exhale, his evident tension releasing all at once. "Thank you, my dearest Emma. Thank you, thank you." In a moment, he was on his knees beside me, kissing my hand.

"I will devote my life to making sure you do not regret your decision."

But I could not think of regrets at that moment. Giddy anticipation seized me, and I felt sure I had made the right choice. To travel to Northwood Abbey! To meet Lord Vairnruth himself! The future was nothing to me. I cared only for the moment, and the moment was sure to be a splendid one.

4

We set out a few days later, the five of us packed into Edgar's carriage with our trunks lashed to the roof. As well as Edgar, Charlotte, and Francis, Sarah travelled with us as a maid for myself and my sister. I was aglow with happiness and hope as we approached Lord Vairnruth's home. Beyond the carriage's tiny window, the striking Derbyshire countryside rolled by, its breathtaking peaks and crags so wild and uncompromising. No wonder a great poet such as Vairnruth chose to live here. If I lived amongst such natural splendour, I was sure I would write poetry every day.

"Emma." Edgar nudged me. "Look that way."

Glancing past him, I caught my breath. Northwood Abbey—a renovated medieval monastery—stood on the opposite side of the valley, framed by a forest like the backdrop of a theatre. Built of golden sandstone, the Abbey glowed beneath the sun. Parts of the church had been left to fall into picturesque ruin, huge windows empty of glass with only the green of the forest behind them, giving the place an air of medieval mystery.

Approaching closer, we came upon a vast, clear lake opposite the house, which mirrored a perfect reflection of its spires. Nearby a peacock wandered, spreading its feathers in a resplendent display. I had never seen such a creature except in drawings, and I stared unabashedly until the carriage came to a halt just outside the house's old oak door.

As Edgar helped me down from my seat, a footman emerged to greet us. He bowed and led us into a narrow stone hallway. Our footsteps echoed off the flagstones. Medieval tapestries adorned the walls, and here and there, ebony furniture was scattered haphazardly. There was a chill in the dusty air, a sense of history around us like a weight. A whisper of ghosts.

Emerging from the darkness, we entered a high-ceilinged hall where sunlight streamed through a large stained-glass window, spilling colour across the bare stone floor. The footman bade us wait, and my heart fluttered as I wondered whether Lord Vairnruth himself was about to appear. But instead, a young woman emerged through one of the doors. She was full-figured and rosy-cheeked, with cherubic blonde ringlets. Edgar's face brightened when he saw her.

"Lady Louisa!"

"Edgar!" Lady Louisa approached him with her hands outstretched. He took them, and they kissed one another's cheeks. "How long has it been?"

"Years. You were just a girl when I saw you last, your Ladyship."

"Oh, call me Louisa, please. We *are* practically family, after all. I'm simply devastated that you've avoided us for so long."

Edgar looked sheepish. "Life rushes by. You know how it is."

"Oh, hardly." Louisa raised her eyes to the ceiling. "I am trapped here day in, day out. Time is as slow as a glacier. Anyway," she turned to the group at large, "I am honoured to meet you all. My name is Louisa Vairnruth; my brother asked me to receive you in his absence. He sends his apologies: he was called away on business this morning and plans to return by dusk."

My heart sank. So I would have to wait a little longer to meet his Lordship. It wasn't the end of the world, but my anticipation had grown to such an extent that it felt like a huge blow. I bit my lip and forced myself to meet Lady Louisa's eyes as she greeted me.

"This is my fiancée," Edgar said. "Miss Emma Crawford."

I curtsied. "Delighted to make your acquaintance, your Ladyship."

"And you!" Louisa flashed me a sly smile. "It will be a pleasure to have someone of my own age here. My brother's friends are dreadful bores."

"I can hardly imagine that to be the case." I shyly returned her smile.

"Oh, wait until you meet them," Louisa replied. "Then you may judge. They are all out hunting, but you shall meet them at dinner. In the meantime, the maid will show you to your rooms so you may make yourselves comfortable."

She took her leave from us, and Charlotte turned to me with a barely concealed look of distaste on her face.

"They say Lady Louisa is a person of loose morals, just like her brother," she whispered as soon as her Ladyship was out of earshot. "You would do well to keep your distance."

VAIRNRUTH'S MAID showed me to a spacious bedroom. Small, arched windows looked out upon the lawn and the lake beyond. At one end of the room stood a four-poster bed hung with velvet curtains and laid with an embroidered bedspread. The overall effect was one of sumptuous riches from a long-ago age.

"I shall feel like a medieval princess in here," I sighed to Sarah, heading straight for the window to look out upon the grounds. The peacock strutted up and down the lawn, chest puffed out, while a little brown peahen picked at the ground, barely raising her head even when he cawed. My heart fluttered at the thought that soon—this very evening—I would meet Lord Vairnruth himself, and on an impulse I hurried to my trunk to make sure I had remembered my copy of *The Water Nymph*.

Sure enough, it was there, nestled between two of my dresses for safekeeping. I placed it on the nightstand beside the bed. I had read it so many times that I felt I already knew the heart of the person who wrote it, even though I'd never met him before. Lord Vairnruth might have been known for his decadent, philandering ways, but I was convinced that someone capable of creating such beauty must be a person of rare insight and empathy. The rumours of immorality were surely exaggerated. I hoped to find someone with whom I could discuss art and poetry for hours.

Sarah helped me to change and freshen up. Anticipation heightened my nerves, and when I headed down for dinner, I felt so sick I was sure I would not be able to eat a single thing. Edgar met me on the stairs, and I was glad of his steadying arm.

"You will be pleased to see your old friend again, I suppose?" I asked as we descended together.

"Very," Edgar replied, but his tone was flat. He sounded as nervous as I was.

In the dining room we found a party of two dozen people, Charlotte and Francis among them, gathered around a vast antique table. Stags' heads frowned down upon us from the wall, and a blazing fire lent the room an edge of warmth against the cool of the oncoming night. As we took our places behind the last remaining seats, I noticed that at the head of the table stood an empty chair. Lady Louisa sat to its right, looking pristine in gold silk, her cheeks flushed by the fire's heat. She was like a perfect doll, with her dark eyes and rose-pink lips, and it occurred to me that all the men in the room must surely be in love with her. Had I been a man, I was sure *I* would have been.

"His Lordship must not have made it home in time for dinner," Edgar muttered beneath the chatter of the other guests. I sensed his disappointment—indeed, I felt it myself. Would we even see his Lordship tonight?

As the first course was served, I looked around the table, taking in the people who were to be my companions for the next few days. The ladies all wore their finest silk gowns, with jewels and feathers in their hair, and I felt distinctly out of place in my simple dress. Judging from the conversation, most of them were well acquainted, and they seemed to have spent the summer flitting from one house to another. To them, this was just another party in a season filled with balls and outings. Several knew Francis and Charlotte, and some recognised Edgar, but aside from a few polite words of small talk, nobody said much to me.

After we were finished eating, the ladies left the men to their cigars and brandy, and headed to the drawing room. There, all was dust and confusion. Part of the wall was still in the process of being re-plastered, and half the chairs were covered by tarpaulin.

"You see what I have to endure?" Lady Louisa gestured at the chaos. She took a seat by the fire and patted the space beside her. "Augustus grew tired of the renovations, and so one day he simply sent the workmen away. He said the noise gave him pain in his temples, and he couldn't bear it any longer. And now I have to live in a building site, with no end to it in sight. You see?"

"I see," I said, sitting down.

"You haven't spent much time in society, I think, Miss Crawford?"

"I have rarely been away from my father's home," I admitted.

Louisa's eyes widened. "And what a place to start your travels."

"I fear this will be where I end them, too," I replied. "After your brother's ball, I am obliged to return home directly for my wedding to Edgar."

"And you truly intend to marry him? Not," Louisa added with an innocent look, "that there is anything wrong with Mr Goodwin, of course. Good by name and by nature. But la! Miss Crawford, such a pretty thing as you shouldn't be in a hurry to throw yourself away on the first man who asks."

I blushed at the idea that she thought me pretty. "Perhaps you might try explaining that to my father."

"Oh, of course I know little of fathers," Louisa replied. "Augustus and I have been orphans these past ten years."

"I'm so sorry for your loss."

"Our father was no loss at all." Louisa waved my concern away. "Our mother, perhaps, but she died when we were too little to remember her. Disadvantages to being orphaned there may be, but at least it means we have no parents to quarrel with about whom we do or do not marry. Augustus has his own fortune, and I am subject only to his whims. But in some ways I suppose I envy you, having someone to look out for your well-being."

I didn't know how to reply to that, so I only smiled. After a moment's silence I said, "Do you expect your brother back this evening?"

"Perhaps." Louisa looked as though she couldn't have cared less one way or the other. "Augustus is always rushing off on errands these days, but to do it the day before his own birthday party, leaving me in charge of all his guests, seems the height of rudeness." She paused. "I hope you don't mind me unburdening myself, my dear Miss Crawford. Only, you know, we are the only people here under twenty, and so I feel we ought to be friends. Don't you think?"

"Of course." I smiled, and Louisa squeezed my hand, her fingers lingering a little longer than seemed quite proper.

"You can't imagine how glad I am to have some female company in this house," she said. "Augustus is *never* in good spirits, nowadays." She heaved a great sigh. "His foul mood infects us all."

I did not know how to respond. "I am sorry to hear that."

"You're a reader," Louisa said. "You have read my brother's poems, I suppose."

"Of course."

"And what do they tell you?" She examined me earnestly. "About him? I tried to read *The Bride of Earnshaw Hall* once and I couldn't make head nor tail of it."

"When I read *The Bride of Earnshaw Hall* I had the impression of ... of someone of great depth and feeling. Not at all like ..."

"Like the Augustus Vairnruth you have heard gossiped about?"

I hesitated. "I suppose not."

"It is all show," Louisa said, casting her gaze around the half-finished room. "I do not know what is behind it, but the front is all show."

5

That night on retiring to bed, I opened my copy of *The Water Nymph*. The world around me fell away as I dove into the magical fever dream of Vairnruth's poetry. The story's ancient setting felt so much closer as I sat in a room that had once belonged to a medieval monk, history and ghosts lurking in the walls all around me.

The story's heroine, a young maiden named Ondine, lived in an isolated village, hemmed with the Alps on one side and a dense forest on the other. Ondine's favourite place to walk was by a lake in the mountains, as round and silver as the moon. One night she stumbled upon a strange man swimming: tall, flaxen-haired, with tanned skin and golden eyes that glowed in the moonlight. The Faerie King himself. Fascinated and enraptured by this strange, beautiful gentleman, Ondine followed him into the water. The next part always made my heart race and my imagination run wild as the beautiful stranger seduced the innocent Ondine, wrapping his arms around her, whispering honeyed, passionate words in her ear.

A sound caught my attention, jolting me out of my reverie. Horses' hooves on gravel. I placed my book on the pillow and crept to look out of the window. A lone man in a dark travelling cloak made his way up the driveway on a black stallion, a hood obscuring his face. Moments later a pair of horses followed, pulling a cart loaded with a large crate. The lone horseman hopped off the horse's back and pushed back his hood, revealing curly black hair and a youthful visage. I stared, my heart hammering. It was difficult to tell from this distance, but surely it could be none other than the master of the house, Lord Vairnruth himself. With his large dark eyes, full lips, and porcelain skin, he was the image of his famous portrait.

Instead of continuing toward the stables, the cart turned off the driveway and trundled down the grass, heading for the lake. Vairnruth followed, and I watched them unload the crate close to the water's edge. It was too far away for me to make it out clearly, but I was sure I saw something silvery slither out into the water and disappear.

The delivery made, Vairnruth trudged back up the grass towards the front door. Then just as he was about to go inside, he paused and looked up directly at me.

With a sharp intake of breath, I fled from the window, my cheeks burning. Had he seen me watching him? And in nothing but my flimsy nightgown, too. As if I could somehow hide my shame in retrospect, I dove beneath my blankets and extinguished the candle. Staring into darkness as my panic gradually subsided, I tried to recall his exact image, a delightful shiver running down my spine. The way he'd looked as he jumped from his magnificent horse. The way he'd pushed back his hood to reveal those famous curls. Lord Vairnruth! I couldn't keep from grinning.

But what had been in the crate? A million possibilities revolved around my mind. The most logical explanation seemed to be some sort of supplies for the party, and yet, why would they be delivered in the dead of night, under cover of such secrecy? And into the water, as well? A surprise for the guests, perhaps? My excitement grew as I wondered what magnificent delights might be in store.

Tomorrow, I thought—tomorrow I would surely meet the poet himself. I could only pray he would not know it was me who had been watching him.

I dreamed I was Ondine, before she was cursed. A girl just like me, with a heart that beat, and blood that rushed through her veins, hot and strong. A girl with lungs that breathed air, two feet that stood on the soil, and a body that longed for touch. For love.

A girl dreaming of escape.

I stood on the shore of a secluded lake. Nestled in a dip surrounded by craggy rocks, it was clear and calm and perfectly round. The Moon Lake. All alone beneath the glow of the moon, I slipped off my dress. My hair was long and golden, my body sensuously curved. I dove into the water and swam, revelling in my nakedness, my freedom. Living among a small community, I felt myself continually watched. Only here, unobserved, could I be myself. Floating on the surface of the water, I let myself be caressed by the moonlight and the touch of my own hands, my nerves aflame as I learned the contours of my body.

Breathless and dripping after my swim, I exited the water and lay on the shore. But as I let the warm night breeze dry my skin, instinct warned me I was being observed. It was as though the night itself had opened its eyes and was watching me. I froze, breath steaming in the cool night air, fearing that one of the village boys had followed me.

Amidst the velvety depths of the night, a movement caught my attention. I sat up. Shining from the darkness between the trees was a pair of golden eyes. Then, gradually, a man emerged from the shadows as though he had been a part of them, shedding them like a second skin.

As the darkness fell away the sharp lines of his face took form. He had a majestic beauty, almost feminine, all high cheekbones and luminous, moon-bright skin. I was instantly in awe of him, the way one might be of a wild predator, and I shrank back as he approached, wishing I had something to cover myself with. There was something dangerous in his welcoming smile, the glint of his too-white teeth.

He was as naked as I, tan-skinned and golden-haired, with eyes that shone like sunbeams, and a smirk on his lips. I knew him from the stories I'd been told as a child. The warnings, the reason why girls were not permitted to stray too far alone. Wayward women who did not do as they were told were at risk of being approached by the Faerie King, who would enchant them with a mere glance, and spirit them away to his realm.

All this rushed through my mind as I wrapped my arms around my legs and stared. My head told me to be afraid, but my body longed for him. For his touch, his beauty. He met my gaze and a thrill shuddered through me. As he approached, I shrugged off my inhibitions and stood to meet him.

I was ready to be enchanted.

6

<hr>

$\mathcal{I}$ slept poorly that night, plagued by feverish dreams. As the weak early-morning sunlight slunk through my bedroom window, I gave up the attempt to rest. Rising, I wrapped my robe around me and went to look outside. Already the sky was a bright cornflower blue, reflected in the placid lake. The peacocks, like me, were already awake, and their caws rang out across the lawn.

I recalled what Louisa had said about her brother the night before: *It is all show. I do not know what is behind it, but the front is all show.* It seemed that even she did not know him well. Indeed, to think that *she* had asked me my impressions of him, based upon his poetry. As though, as a reader, I might have some sort of additional insight that was barred to her. His own sister!

I wondered if it were possible.

Sarah was surprised to see me already up when she came in to stoke the fire.

"Miss," she said, sounding quite put out, "why are you sitting by the window? You'll catch your death of cold."

"It is not cold," I remonstrated. "See, the day is sunny already."

"In this old place it seems always cold to me." Sarah shivered. "Last night I felt I should never get warm. Some of his lordship's servants say the place is haunted. I should not be surprised, Miss, if they were right. Just think of all the miserable old monks who used to roam these halls. Why would anyone want to live in such a place?"

"Sarah, you do let your tongue run on dreadfully." I went to pick out a dress from my wardrobe. "Don't you think the place has a certain charm? A picturesqueness?"

"I shouldn't know, Miss," Sarah replied, gloomily. "I only know that it is cold."

Once dressed, I went downstairs for breakfast, but found the dining room and the parlour both empty. Concluding that it was still too early for Louisa and her friends to descend, I decided to go in search of a library, hoping for somewhere to sit and read while I waited.

The old monastery was a rabbit warren of tight corridors and small rooms, and I wandered for some time, nervously pushing open door after door, only to discover areas still left un-renovated and in disarray. But eventually I came to the library, a large, airy, pleasant room at the front of the house. The walls on three sides were lined with bookshelves, while bay windows overlooked the lake. In the centre of the room stood a hefty oak desk, covered in books and papers, and suddenly it hit me: I was in *Lord Vairnruth's* library. This was his desk. Those were his papers.

Tentatively, I approached the desk, not meaning to pry, only to cast an eye over what was there, perhaps catch a glimpse of his handwriting. A cursory examination told me that most of the books were volumes of folklore and history, many of them dealing with German legends of the medieval period. The papers were covered with dashed-off scribbles, peppered by ink blots, as though they had been written in a frantic hurry. Curious, I leaned closer, trying to make out some of the words. To my fascination, they seemed to relate to *The Water Nymph*—or at least, the myth that had inspired the poem. Picking over them, I found an eye-witness account of the sighting of a woman in a lake in Germany, accompanied by a map that claimed to show the exact location where she could be found. My breath caught, my imagination immediately running away with me. Was it possible the nymph could be real?

"Do you find anything to please you, madam?"

I jumped at the unexpected voice, and flinched back from the desk as though I had been caught in a criminal act. A tall, dark-haired figure stood in the doorway. Lord Vairnruth himself. He wore a red printed dressing gown, one hand tucked in a pocket as he regarded me with an amused smile.

"I'm so sorry." My cheeks burned. "I wasn't meaning to— I mean, I didn't see ..." I took a deep breath. "I am interrupting, sir. I will show myself out."

I took a few steps, intending to do just that, before I realised that Vairnruth was blocking the only doorway, and I stopped, feeling stupid, in the middle of the floor.

"There's no need for that." Vairnruth gestured for me to sit down by the fireplace. "Please stay, make yourself comfortable, Mrs ...?"

"Miss," I stammered, taking my seat. "Emma Crawford."

"A pleasure to make your acquaintance, Miss Crawford." Vairnruth seated himself across from me.

I bowed my head, at a loss for what to say. I had known Lord Vairnruth's face from his portrait for some time, but not even my glimpse of him the night before had been enough to prepare me for his presence in reality. At first, I was only aware of his sheer physicality, compared with the hazy jumble of brushstrokes and imagination that had represented him in my mind. I realised what I had pictured was a mere shade of the real man: a moon to his sun. Augustus Vairnruth in the flesh was an embodiment of charismatic power and raw energy: his bright, dark eyes; the nonchalant way he pushed his curly hair back from his forehead; the slight, feminine pout of his full lips, at odds with his undeniably masculine build. He was tall and lean, with strong shoulders and a crooked nose. His air of coiled masculinity made me feel like a small, timid mouse, and he a predator waiting to strike.

This was not the man of my fantasies. This was a real man, a stranger to me, and what was more, a stranger with a reputation for excess, seduction, womanising. And I was here with him, alone, while the rest of the house slept.

I was glad Charlotte could not see inside my mind at that moment. How smug she would be at my sudden discomfort! I cast my gaze at the floor and clasped my hands like a schoolgirl.

"And did you?" Vairnruth asked.

I looked up, confused. "Excuse me?"

"Did you find anything to please you?" He gestured to the desk. "Amongst my writings?"

"I ... I saw nothing of it. But all your writing pleases me, sir. Everything I have read of yours is exquisite."

A flicker of amusement crossed his face—or was it pleasure? "Exquisite, indeed? In that case, you must stay and take some tea with me before breakfast."

He got up to ring the bell, and after a moment a maid appeared. Her evident surprise at finding me there made me blush.

"Some tea, please," Vairnruth said. "Earl Grey, with lemon."

The maid bobbed a curtsey and departed. We sat in awkward silence for a few moments until she returned with our tea—at least, *I* sat in awkward silence, perched in my armchair. Vairnruth seemed quite at his ease, lounging with one ankle hooked over the other knee, watching me.

"You are here for the ball, I take it?" he said, once our tea was served.

"Yes," I replied. "With Edgar Goodwin. My fiancé." I couldn't help but blush as I said the words.

"Ah yes, I remember. The old fellow said he would be bringing someone." Vairnruth narrowed his eyes. "He didn't tell me you were so pretty, though. Whatever convinced you to betroth yourself to that bore? It seems an awful waste."

Irritation prickled me. "Sir, need I remind you that you are speaking of my fiancé?"

"No, no, indeed. I am terribly sorry. That was disrespect-ful." His expression was solemn, but I couldn't shake the feeling that he was laughing at me.

I took a sip of my tea. "You were friends with Edgar at Cambridge, were you not?"

"'Friends' might be somewhat overstating our relation-ship, but yes, I knew him."

"Well enough to invite him to your birthday ball," I pressed. "Why would you do that, if you were not friends?"

Vairnruth gave me a shrewd look. "What has he told you about me, Miss Crawford?"

"Nothing!" I said quickly, thinking of the hints Edgar had dropped. The possibility that there might have been some-thing *more* to their relationship, at least on Edgar's side. "He has said very little."

"Nothing," Vairnruth sat back in his seat, "is not the same thing as very little."

I had the feeling my questioning had perturbed him some-what, yet my curiosity was piqued, and so I persisted: "You still haven't explained why you invited him."

"Perhaps because he told me he would be bringing a

certain Miss Emma Crawford with him." Vairnruth broke into a grin.

"Nonsense," I replied. "You had not heard of me before."

"Hadn't I?" He shifted seats to sit beside me, close enough that our thighs almost touched.

"You are trying to disconcert me, sir," I said, a little breathless.

"Am I?" He pushed a strand of hair away from my face, and his fingers grazed my cheek. "Is it so hard to believe that news of your beauty has travelled as far as Derbyshire?"

He was laughing at me now, I could tell. Amusement danced in his eyes. He must have realised it was me watching him the night before, and come to some unflattering conclusion about my virtue as a result. Why else would he tease me so? My cheeks flushed; tears sprung to my eyes. I put down my cup and got to my feet, turning away so that he would not see my humiliation.

"It must be almost time for breakfast," I said. "Edgar will be wondering where I am." And before Lord Vairnruth could give any kind of answer, I hurried out of the room.

7

*C*onfused and shaken, I paused for a moment in the hallway to compose myself before heading into the breakfast room where the company was finally beginning to gather. A vast spread had been set out: meats and cheeses, eggs cooked in all sorts of different ways, coffee, cocoa, and pastries. I had never seen anything quite so extravagant, just for breakfast.

"Lord Vairnruth has spent so much time on the continent, he seems to have brought back some of their customs," Charlotte said as I took a seat beside her.

"Has he travelled a great deal then?" Francis asked.

"I understand he spent much of last summer in Germany," Edgar interjected from across the table, just as Lady Louisa entered.

"*All* summer." She sat down with a theatrical sigh. "I was insufferably bored here all by myself."

"Surely there must be any number of families who would be happy to have you stay with them for the summer, your Ladyship?" Edgar said.

Louisa smiled and started to spread a croissant with

butter. "My brother preferred me to stay at home. He is my only guardian, you know, and I was still under-age at the time, so I was compelled to obey."

"But why? What on Earth would be the purpose of leaving you stuck here all alone?"

Seeing him reach for the coffee pot, I said, "Ought we not to wait until his Lordship comes down?"

Faces turned in my direction. Louisa gave a small laugh.

"My brother never comes down in time for breakfast," she said. "Indeed, I'm not even sure he is home yet."

"I—" I had been about to say I had seen him, but something stopped me. Instead I only nodded and poured myself some cocoa. As the conversation continued around me, I ruminated over Vairnruth's manner towards me. His teasing had confounded me—I wasn't sure whether to take it as flattering, or contemptuous. On the one hand, he had implied that I was a beauty, worthy of note. On the other, he had clearly been laughing at me. Was I merely the butt of some private joke of his? And he was ill-mannered enough to call my own fiancé a bore, right in front of me.

The more I thought about it, the more angry I became. I began to wish I hadn't met Lord Vairnruth; that I had never come to Northwood Abbey at all. It hurt me to think that my precious *Water Nymph*, and all those other volumes I so adored, would now be tainted by my knowledge of their author's rudeness.

Just as my fury reached fever pitch, and I was seriously considering asking Edgar to take me home, the door opened and in strode Vairnruth himself, much to the surprise of everyone except me. He flung himself down in the empty seat at the top of the table, bringing with him a cloud of ill-temper, and helped himself to boiled eggs and kippers without a single word to anybody.

"La, Augustus!" Louisa exclaimed. "You frightened me out of my wits! I had thought you were not home."

"Lolly, your voice is dreadfully shrill." Her brother winced. "You sound like a fishwife."

"Oh, I suppose he has another of his headaches," Louisa said. "He's ever so tedious about it. All in the house must be complete silence, and we all walk around as if on eggshells so as not to disturb him."

"You never walked on eggshells in your life, Lolly." Vairnruth knocked the top off his boiled egg with rather more force than was warranted. I wondered what had happened to put him in such a bad humour since we had spoken. "You don't know the meaning of the word 'silence'."

Louisa laughed, her golden curls quivering. "Listen to him! He always goes on like this. His nerves! His head! He can't concentrate, can't think straight. Why, he's as fragile as any lady. How he managed at Cambridge, I've no idea." She turned to her brother. "I suppose you got home very late last night?"

"That's right."

"Well, aren't you even going to speak to your new guests? Sir Frances and Lady Melrose are here, you see. And Lady Melrose's sister, Miss Crawford. And Edgar, of course."

Vairnruth nodded at us each in turn, unsmiling, betraying no sign that he had seen me before.

"My apologies for not being here to greet you yesterday," he said. "I was called away on unavoidable business." Then he lapsed into silence for the rest of the meal. Every now and then I looked up to see him gazing out of the window with a melancholy aspect, appearing not to hear a word as the rest of the party gossiped. Once breakfast was over, he retreated to his library, and Louisa proposed a walk around the Abbey grounds for the rest of us.

"I am terribly sorry for my brother's rudeness," she said as we donned our bonnets. Apparently, we were firm friends by now, and Louisa insisted on tying my ribbons for me—a gesture of intimacy I found rather endearing. "His moods are somewhat ... mercurial."

"I have heard it said that creative people can be temperamental," I replied, trying to be as diplomatic as possible. The idea of asking Edgar to take me home hadn't left my thoughts, but for reasons I couldn't quite explain to myself, I had hesitated to speak to him, telling myself first that I would do it after breakfast, and then that I would perhaps stay long enough to at least take in the grounds. The acuteness of the wound Vairnruth had inflicted upon me had already begun to dull, my original fascination returning as I ruminated on his strange change of mood. Could it have anything to do with the crate I had seen delivered the night before? I couldn't get my mind off the thing I had seen slither into the lake.

The ball was due to take place the following evening, and as we walked out onto the driveway, Louisa's arm linked through mine, I saw that preparations were already underway. A large marquee stood on the main lawn, and some of the servants were decorating it with garlands, while others unloaded crates and barrels from a nearby cart.

"Will the party be outside, then?" I asked.

Louisa smiled. "'Tis a midsummer masquerade. Of course it must be outside!"

"A masquerade!" I stopped walking and turned to her. "Ought I to have a costume?"

"La, Edgar!" Louisa waved to him, far ahead. "Did you not tell Miss Crawford?"

"Tell Miss Crawford what?" Edgar called back.

"That she ought to have a costume for tomorrow night! Good Lord, you men are not to be trusted with anything." Louisa turned back to me and patted my arm. "Not to worry. We shall find you something."

THAT EVENING'S dinner was even more sumptuous than the last. The summer night was warm enough that Louisa ordered the dining table to be carried outside onto a patio, and with Lord Vairnruth finally at its head, the company came alive. The spread was as lavish as could be desired, and I found my wine glass topped up so frequently that I couldn't keep track of how much I had consumed.

"I've eaten so much, I'm afraid I might burst," I told Edgar, laughing, as the servants cleared away the remains of the main course. They replaced the empty dishes with full ones: jellies and cakes, custards and puddings. Louisa plucked a honeyed fig from a silver platter and ate it, licking the honey from her fingers one by one with a dainty pink tongue. Then she declared she could stomach no more and stood, suggesting a walk down to the lakeside.

"Nobody wants to go down there at this time of night," Vairnruth replied. He had been merry all evening, but now his visage darkened as though his sister's idea displeased him.

"Nonsense! Miss Crawford will come, won't you? And Edgar?"

"We will all go," Charlotte declared hastily, shooting me a glance. No doubt she didn't trust me to be left alone with the others.

And so we trooped down to the water's edge, tipsy and cheerful in the evening's fading light.

"There's magic in the air," I said. "I can taste it."

Louisa caught my words and smiled. "Come, Miss Crawford. Let us dip our toes in the water."

She ran down the lawn, pulling me after her, whooping and laughing. By the time we reached the lake, I was laughing too. She came to a stop so abruptly that I almost collided with her; she caught me, and we stood holding one another, trying to catch our breath through fits of giggles. Grinning, I looked into her face, and my heart stopped. With the colour high in her cheeks, and her eyes glittering with mirth, she was so breathtakingly pretty that for a moment I could do nothing but stare.

"My dear Miss Crawford," she said, "I'm so glad you came."

Somewhere behind her smile I sensed the loneliness she had felt before my arrival. I couldn't quite understand why, but my being here meant something to her, and that endeared her to me.

On the lake's shore, Louisa slipped off her shoes and indicated I should do the same. As I placed my feet on the cool stones, the others caught us up.

"It will be cold," Lord Vairnruth warned. "Miss Crawford will catch her death."

"Augustus, whenever did you become such a bore? Come along, Miss Crawford." And she led me to the lake's edge.

Vairnruth was right: it was ice cold, and I flinched when my toes touched the water, but I braced myself and picked up my skirts, following Louisa until we were ankle deep. The lake lay ahead of us, calm and shining in the sunset, and I wished desperately that I could plunge in and swim to my heart's content.

"Emma! Whatever are you doing?"

At the sound of Charlotte's voice I turned back, but not before I saw a flicker of silver pass beneath the lake's surface. I looked again and it was gone.

"What was that?" I asked.

"What?" Louisa said, but before I could answer, Lord Vairnruth reached for my arm, drawing me gently out of the water.

"Come, Miss Crawford. Let us go back to the house before you catch cold."

His fingers were hot on my bare skin, and my stomach somersaulted at his sudden closeness. Louisa brushed past us, her mood suddenly irritable as she scooped up her shoes and stormed back towards the house. Lord Vairnruth offered me his arm and we followed, but his steps grew slower and slower, and soon we were hanging back well behind the others.

"What did you see beneath the water?" he asked me.

"I'm not sure. Something silver. A fish, I suppose."

"I suppose so." He glanced back, and his voice hardened. "There's nothing in there of note, I can assure you."

8

---

othing in there of note.

Vairnruth's words returned to me as I sat at my bedroom window later that night, sipping cocoa with a blanket around my shoulders. I did not believe him. I was transfixed by the water. I longed to know what was beneath its surface. What had been in the crate I'd seen delivered the night before?

By candlelight, I picked up my copy of *The Water Nymph* again, wanting to sink into the mind of the man I'd spent the day with. I wanted to understand him, to read his thoughts— and how lucky, I thought, that I could do just that.

I turned to the page after Ondine's seduction by the Faerie King, in which he invites her to join him in his realm. The lake, it turns out, is a portal, and they swim together beneath the surface and into the land of Faerie, a world of pure indulgence, where love is revered above all else and nothing is prohibited—except one thing. Inside a cage of coloured glass, the Faerie King keeps a golden feather which Ondine is forbidden to touch.

Curling my legs up beneath me, I read long into the night,

savouring every word of Vairnruth's delicious poetry. Travelling Faerie alongside her beautiful prince, Ondine discovers appetites that she didn't know she had, pleasures that she hardly dreamed possible. She plucks a round, ripe fruit from a silver tree and devours it, delirious with ecstasy as the king watches on.

The thought of losing my inhibitions so, of coming undone in the presence of such a beautiful creature, made my cheeks grow warm and my stomach flutter. I wanted ... but I hardly knew what I wanted, that was the trouble. I had no idea what would sate this hunger inside me.

And then I saw him—that dark figure again, just as I had the night before, but this time he was leaving the house, not entering. In the clear moonlight, I watched him cross the driveway and head down the lawn towards the lake.

The lake.

Curiosity battled with my better judgement, and won. Jumping to my feet, I grabbed my travelling cloak and threw it on over my nightgown, making sure to put the hood up so that no-one might see my face. Then I hurried out of my room and downstairs, sneaking out of the heavy front door into the night.

Cool air chilled my blazing cheeks as I ran down the lawn. I could no longer see the figure I assumed was Vairnruth, and I hoped I had not lost him completely. But as I approached the lake, I spotted his silhouette on the shore, and slipped behind a tree to watch him throw off his cloak. He stripped to his undershirt and breeches, and to my astonishment, he dove into the water, vanishing beneath the surface.

He was gone for so long that I began to worry, and then to panic. Had something gone wrong? Was he drowning? Should I do something? I was lucky that I could swim a little, having been taught by my father in the pond near our home, but I was nowhere near strong enough to assist a grown man, should he need rescuing.

Still, the seconds ticked by, each one an eternity, and my heart was in my mouth as I deliberated between throwing myself into the water after him, and running back to the house for help. Then—thank God—he surfaced.

And immediately spotted me watching him.

In my fear I had stepped out of my hiding place, and I was not quick enough to conceal myself again. I stood utterly immobile, fixed in Vairnruth's gaze as he swam back to shore and walked, dripping, out of the water.

"You are a curious one, Miss Crawford," he said, his voice a little taut from the cold. "Always watching. Always where you're not expected to be."

I could not speak, even to apologise. The words caught in my throat, and I merely stared as he threw his cloak back around his shoulders and brushed past me, clearly in an ill humour. He took a few brisk strides up the lawn, then stopped, turning back.

"Tell me something, Miss Crawford," he said.

"Y-yes?"

"You have read my stories. My poems. Am I what you expected?"

I opened my mouth, then closed it again. I had no idea how to answer, nor what sort of response he was expecting from me.

"You are not," I managed at last.

Vairnruth's lip curled. "You came here wanting to meet a poet, and you found a brute, didn't you? A worthless rake who is cruel to his sister. And what is worse—I cannot even write anymore. I don't deserve your admiration, Miss Crawford, so take it, and yourself, back home where you belong."

"What do you mean, you can't write anymore?"

He walked away, but I hurried to keep up with him.

"I am empty. A mere shell. I have not been able to write a word. Not since—" He glanced at the lake. "Not since I returned from my last visit to Germany. So you see, madam, your disappointment is justified."

"I'm not disappointed," I protested. "Indeed, how could I be? We barely know each other." Suddenly bold, I put a hand on his arm. "Won't you talk to me. Perhaps I can help?"

He stopped to stare, as if seeing me anew. "Help? There's nothing to help." Bitterness crept into his voice. "I have chased after worthless dreams for so long that now there's nothing left of me. Now, get inside the house before you freeze to death."

"Wait. I have to know. How did you stay under the water for so long?"

Vairnruth looked at me for a long moment, then shook his head and walked into the Abbey.

I dreamed of the Faerie King again. Sitting beside me on the lake shore, he told me stories. Stories not just of the wonders of this world, but of others, too. Stories where reality slipped away like a curtain being pushed out of view, and in its place emerged a magical realm—his realm, a land of glittering towers and silver seas and trees hung with precious stones instead of fruit. His words wove a web around my heart and I was enraptured.

"Will you take me there?" I asked him.

"I will," he agreed, "on one condition."

"What's that?"

"You become mine, body and soul. You must promise you will come with me, obey only me, stay in my realm and never return."

When I hesitated, thinking of my family, my friends—all I would leave behind—the Faerie King laid me on the sand and kissed his way down my body, the velvety touch of his tongue making me weak.

"Swear you'll be mine."

What could I do? He promised me the world, pleasures untold, until desire bloomed within me like a spring flower.

"I'll be yours."

9

Sometimes, I would pause in my reading of *The Water Nymph* during the section where Ondine was still discovering the pleasures of Faerie and her new lover. Those stanzas of the poem were a gorgeous dream, and I never wanted the fantasy to end. If I shut the book and walked away, Ondine could stay in that delirious state forever, her happiness unsullied by reality. But that was not how the story ended, and I knew I would always pick it up again eventually, and finish the book.

I sat on the lawn in the sunshine, beneath the looming shadow of the Abbey, my fingers clutched around my closed book as I watched the servants prepare the marquee for that night's ball. I hadn't seen Vairnruth all morning, yet I longed to catch a glimpse of him. My head swirled with thoughts of him. Endless questions ran through my mind. What had he been doing in the water so late at night? How had he stayed under so long? What had caused his terrible writer's block, and—the one that preoccupied me the most—what did he mean when he said there was 'nothing left of him'?

My imagination conjured up a story of terrible heartbreak.

A woman had undoubtably spurned him, making him turn away from love and causing a depression that had destroyed his muse. But surely all he needed was the right person to help him regain his faith in womankind? Someone who understood him, who would be devoted to him. I looked down at my book. Someone who knew his heart and his mind as well as her own, already.

Someone just like me.

My heart swelled as I considered the possibility that Lord Vairnruth really was my very own Faerie King, and my cheeks glowed hot as I imagined all the pleasures he might introduce me to. He was, after all, well known for his womanising ways. How many women had he bedded? Surely enough to make him a more than competent lover.

In the distance, I spied Edgar, Francis, and Charlotte taking a walk in the gardens, and felt a pang of guilt. I was engaged to Edgar, now, and I ought not to be indulging in such sinful thoughts about another man. And yet ... Edgar would surely understand. He would never be able to give me what I craved, but Vairnruth—Vairnruth could, if only I could break through the wall of ice he had formed around himself, and make him love me.

Tonight was the ball; in a couple of days we would be leaving for good. I didn't have much time. Spurred by a sudden determination, I got to my feet and strode off in search of Lady Louisa.

I found her lounging in the parlour, nibbling on candied fruits. She was surrounded by admirers, both men and women, all of them vying for her attention with witty remarks, but the moment she saw me she waved them all aside and got up to greet me.

"My dear Miss Crawford! Wherever have you been?" She dragged me over to her chaise and bade me take a seat beside her. Seeing they were no longer wanted, the admirers dispersed.

"Lord, they are so tiresome." Louisa slipped her arm through mine and laid her head on my shoulder. "Like a group of performing parrots." She plucked a candied orange slice from the platter. "Try one of these. They're supposed to be for the party later, but they're so delightful I could not resist." And without waiting for my assent, she popped it in my mouth.

She was right, it was delicious. Sharp and sweet; the most exotic thing I'd ever tasted. Louisa watched me eat, her eyes on my lips, and when I was finished she said, "You have a little sugar, just there."

Leaning in, she swiped the sugar my bottom lip with her tongue. Taken aback, I stiffened, but Louisa only laughed.

"Oh, do not look so frightened, Miss Crawford—or may I call you Emma?—I will not eat you, I promise. Now, did you come to me for a reason?"

"I ..." Bathed in her presence, I forgot myself entirely. She was just as beautiful as her brother, albeit in a softer way, and I found myself longing for her tongue on my lips once more. Picking up another candy, I tried to recollect why I was there. "I would like to ask for your help."

"My help?"

"You mentioned I would need a costume for tonight's ball."

Louisa's eyes lit up. "Of course I did! Well, what shall we dress you as?"

"Can you ..." I hesitated, feeling foolish, but Louisa nodded at me to go on. "Can you make me look beautiful? As much as possible, I mean?"

"Can I?" Louisa laughed, a bright, tinkling laugh. "But my dear Emma, that will be easy." She gave me a shrewd look. "Is there someone whose eye you want to catch? Not your esteemed fiancé, I'm sure."

I shook my head. "I should like to please his Lordship," I admitted, blushing. "He seems unhappy. I thought perhaps I could ..."

"... Raise his spirits?" Louisa's smile was wry. "A pretty thing like you is guaranteed to raise more than just his spirits. But are you sure that's what you want? You're such an innocent, Emma." She touched my hair, twirling it with her fingers. My scalp tingled. "My brother devours girls like you for breakfast."

"I do," I said. Then, trying to inject some greater confidence into my voice: "It's what I want."

"Well, then! We will see what we can do."

LATER THAT DAY, I sat perched on Lady Louisa's satin-curtained bed as she rummaged in her wardrobe, pulling out dress after dress and flinging them onto the quilt beside me.

"No," she muttered, "no, that's not quite it. That will not do at all. This one, perhaps? ... No, certainly not."

She had more dresses than I had ever seen in my life. Silk and organza, embroidered and printed, embellished with lace and sprinkled with jewels. I gazed at each of them as they flew in my direction, amazed that she could treat objects of such beauty so carelessly.

"Ah!" she exclaimed at last. "This is the one."

The dress she held up made my jaw drop. It was crafted in shimmering ivory silk and decorated with fluttering strips of organza in shades of blue and aquamarine. Silver embroidery swirled around the pearls on the bodice, and rather than the usual cap sleeves, it had only thin, pearl-studded straps. The skirt was long, its train pooling on the floor at Louisa's feet.

"You want me to wear that?" I said, breathless with astonishment.

She smiled. "I have a mask and headdress to go with it. They will look perfect on you. And we shall match! The theme of the night is mythical creatures. I am going as the Firebird, from one of Augustus's poems. You will be Ondine, from another."

"Ondine? The Water Nymph? No, I couldn't, surely? I would look ridiculous. Your brother would think me impertinent."

"Certainly not!" Louisa protested. "He likes you, I can tell. And this will be the perfect outfit to attract his notice. That *is* what you wanted, isn't it?" There was a wicked glint in her eye as she laid the gown on the bed. "Now, turn around so I can unbutton your dress."

"Wouldn't you like me to call the maid?"

"No, no, we can manage ourselves, can't we? Turn around."

I turned to face the mirror, and felt Louisa's hands at my back, unfastening my dress. A moment later, she was slipping it off my shoulders. Her fingers grazed my bare skin, leaving goosebumps in their wake. I watched her in the mirror, marvelling once again at how pretty she was, and then her eyes met mine, sending a jolt of lightning through me. My heart beat faster.

Between us, we pulled the dress and petticoats down over my hips, and I stepped out of them and laid them on the bed, now dressed only in my stays and shift.

"You must take those off, too," Louisa told me.

"These?" I glanced at my stays.

"They will spoil the line of the dress. See how thin the silk is?"

Blushing, I let her unlace my stays. I had been undressed by another woman many a time—usually by Sarah, for it was quite usual to be helped by one's maid. But Louisa doing it was quite different, somehow. Before long I stood naked before the looking-glass, Louisa behind me. She met my eyes in the mirror, holding my gaze for a long, lingering moment.

"Pretty girl," she said. "You're wasted on the men."

She bent her head and kissed my neck once, briskly, then helped me into the Ondine costume, adjusting the bodice and pulling the ribbons tight so that my bosom thrust up. The fabric was so sheer that I could see the pink of my nipples through it, and the thought of stepping out in front of the whole company so attired made my stomach flutter.

Turning me to face her, Louisa put her hands on my waist and stepped back to examine me.

"The men will lose their minds when they see you," she said. "But there's something missing." She went to her dressing table to open a carved wooden jewellery box. From it, she withdrew a sparkling necklace, which she fastened around my neck. Then she rummaged in a drawer and found the mask and headdress she had mentioned.

"You ought to wear your hair loose," she said, and without further ado she pulled the pins from my hair, until it fell in dark waves around my shoulders. In it she fixed the pearl-encrusted headdress, then tied the white lace and pearl mask on my face.

"There, now," she said, stepping aside so I could see myself in the mirror. "What do you think? Edgar will never know you."

I stared. She was right. I should not even have recognised myself. I looked like a dark-lashed mystery behind my mask, my lips turned full and sensual from the hint of makeup Louisa had dabbed on them. The low-cut dress exposed an expanse of skin, my breasts high and round, the sparkling diamond of Louisa's necklace nestled between them. And to have my hair flowing loose down my back made me feel strangely free, magical—elated, even.

"Do you like it?" Louisa pressed.

"I—yes."

"Good." Standing behind me, she laid her hand on my waist, leaning in close to my ear. Her soft breath caressed my skin, and I shivered, my every sense alert to her. Her silken touch; her smooth, sensual voice; her sweet, peach-blossom scent.

"Now make yourself comfortable while I get dressed," she said, "and then we shall have some fun."

As I waited for Louisa to choose her outfit, I thought about Ondine's story. Despite having everything she could possibly wish for in Faerie, she became transfixed by the one thing that was barred to her: the golden feather. Whispers from the other fae told her that to touch the feather would be to learn the meaning of true love. Unable to resist the temptation, one night Ondine snuck into the Faerie King's bedchamber as he slept and opened the cage. As she reached for the feather, the King woke. Finding her breaking his single rule, he was so incensed that he threw her out of his realm and wrenched her soul from her body. She was forced to live for all eternity in the lake.

The only way she could escape this fate and gain her soul back, so the poem said, was to find a faithful human man of pure intentions to marry her. And so she lay in wait. Every man who passed her way would be subject to a test: she would seduce them, and if they succumbed to her charms, they failed. Finding them neither pure nor faithful, the nymph would suck out their souls to feed her insatiable hunger.

I examined myself in the mirror, trying to imagine myself as a wicked seductress, caring for nothing and nobody but my own desire. The idea excited me. My heart thudded, and a warmth spread in the depths of my stomach as Louisa began to undress. She was fleshier than I was, all creamy skin and voluptuous curves, with a flirtatious glint in her eye. *If I were a man*, I found myself thinking once again, *I should want to touch her.*

Maybe even kiss her.

My neck still tingled where her lips had touched my skin. When she next spoke, jolting me out of my reverie, I blushed at the wild thoughts that had been running through my mind.

"Well?" she asked. "Do I make a good Firebird?"

Her dress was flame-orange, licked with tongues of red silk. Rubies encircled her throat, and red feathers hid the upper half of her face. Her blonde hair tumbled in waves around the bare skin of her shoulders, framing a bosom that threatened to escape its bounds with her every breath.

"Beautiful," I said, hardly able to tear my eyes away.

Her lips curved into a smile. "I'm glad you think so."

10

*E*vening came, and the driveway grew busy with carriages arriving. Louisa ordered some refreshments, and we sat in her upstairs parlour, watching from the window as guests made their way down the lawn to the marquee, all of them dressed in the most splendid costumes. I saw Edgar, Charlotte, and Francis amongst them, and was eager to join them, but Louisa would not allow it.

"We must make ourselves fashionably late," she insisted. "Later even than Augustus. The two of us together—we shall make an impression. You want to get his attention, and I know just how to do it."

I was anxious to be doing something, aware that precious minutes were ticking by. In my mind's eye, I pictured Lord Vairnruth dancing with other ladies, entertaining one beauty after another, perhaps even finding himself a new muse, while I sat uselessly sipping tea. But I could hardly go down to the party unaccompanied, so I waited until dusk fell, and Louisa declared it time to make our entrance.

In the warm twilight, we left the house and followed the lantern-lit path to the marquee. I could taste the magic in the air, sweet and ripe like a succulent fruit. Passing beneath the tent's flower-garlanded entrance, I felt as though I were stepping into another world, one built out of fantasy and dreams. It was like passing into Faerie.

Beneath the flickering light of dozens of candles, a company of fairy tale creatures danced a cotillion to the music of a string quartet. The woman wore dresses of vivid silk, and feathers in their hair, while the gentlemen were dressed as dashing princes and caped villains. All had their faces hidden by masks—painted ones, hand-held ones, masks with long, sharp noses like beaks. In the centre of it all stood an ice peacock, its carved wings sparkling wetly in the hot night.

Louisa linked her arm with mine and made a point of walking slowly to the head of the room, her shoes tapping on the temporary dance floor. Eyes followed us: with our long hair loose and our skin-baring dresses, we must have looked very wild and unusual even amongst such lavish company. I blushed red-hot and was glad nobody could see my face.

"Now, where is my brother?" Louisa scanned the crowd. "Ah!"

I followed her gaze to see a gentleman in a yellow embroidered frock coat, whose golden mask shone beneath the hot lights. He had run white powder through his hair, disguising its usual dark colour, but still Augustus Vairnruth was unmistakable.

Once she was sure she had her brother's attention, not to mention the rest of the guests, Louisa took my shoulders and turned me to face her.

"Let us give them something to watch," she said, leaning towards me.

No sooner had I realised what she was doing—and caught her peach-blossom scent—than her mouth was on mine, and I froze. My heart thudded. I could not move. Her lips were warm and soft, the kiss delicately sweet—and suddenly over. I was left gasping, my body missing the warmth of her closeness as she darted away to greet her brother.

I was abandoned in the centre of the room, all eyes on me. All of a sudden, I felt I had been cruelly used; that Louisa had not intended to help me, but merely to create a spectacle with herself at the centre. I whirled around, hunting for Charlotte or Edgar, seeing nothing but staring eyes and strange masks at every turn. Louisa hung off Vairnruth's arm, giggling and chattering. He looked in my direction, but I could not tell what expression he wore behind the gold mask. The night felt close, the heat stifling. I was certain I could hear people whispering. Laughing at me.

I would leave, I decided. Go back to the house and hide in my room. Nobody would have to know that the girl Louisa had kissed was me. But there were so many bodies around, so many masked people passing by, that I'd lost sight of the exit. As I wandered, ducking and weaving through the crowd, I became caught in the middle of the dancers, buffeted this way and that like a leaf in the wind. My long skirt got under my feet and I stumbled, only to find myself caught by a strong arm.

I looked up—directly into Lord Vairnruth's golden mask. The reflection of the candles on its bright surface dazzled me, and I had to glance away.

"Are you all right, Miss Crawford?" he asked me.

"How did you—?"

He smiled. "You are not as well disguised as you might imagine."

I blushed hard. "What Lady Louisa did ... I had no idea ... She surprised me."

"My sister likes to make herself controversial." Vairnruth gently led me to the edge of the dance floor. "I am sorry that she coerced you into becoming part of her spectacle."

"It is ..." I sighed, frustrated. "It is nothing more than

what Charlotte warned me about. I should have listened to her. I should—"

"Have what? Stayed at home? Married Mr Goodwin? Moved into his rectory without complaint?"

I studied his face, wondering how much he knew about Edgar's predilections. "It would be a simple life. An easy life. *Will* be," I corrected myself.

"And is that all you want? Truly?"

No, my heart screamed. *I want you*. But my courage failed me, and all I said was, "What else is there?"

"Emma!"

Charlotte forced her way through the sea of guests, her mask pushed up on top of her head, her face red. I was certain she was about to deliver me a lecture about improper behaviour.

Vairnruth saw her approach and extended me a hand covered with jewelled rings. "Dance with me."

After an instant's hesitation, I placed my hand in his, and his warm fingers wrapped around my palm. He led me back amongst the dancers just as another reel began.

Like the ebb and flow of waves, we swirled around each other, coming together then breaking apart, as the dance commanded. For fleeting moments we were close, our fingers touching, his hands lingering on my waist, and then the next thing I knew, we would be at opposite sides of the room.

Once, as he walked me through a turn, Vairnruth leaned in close to my ear and said, "How came you to choose the Ondine costume?"

We broke apart; I was relieved to have a moment to consider my answer.

"I did not," I said, when next we met. "It was Louisa's suggestion."

"The role suits you, but be sure you do not lose yourself in it."

We parted again, and a moment later the music came to an end. Vairnruth bowed to me from the other side of the circle, then disappeared into the crowd, leaving me to wonder what his words meant. Once again, my irritation was piqued: at his mysteriousness; at his sister's teasing. I felt like a mouse being toyed with by a pair of cats.

"Emma."

I blinked and Edgar was at my side, passing me a cup of punch. His brows knitted together in a mirror of my own annoyance, although I could not tell with whom he was angry.

"I see you have decided to throw yourself straight into the inappropriate behaviour." Charlotte waddled over to join us. She was costumed as a fertility goddess, her belly straining against the pale green silk of her dress. "And how do you feel about having made such a dreadful laughing stock of yourself?"

"Laughing stock!" My face flushed, and I took a sip of my punch to hide my upset. Then another.

"Hardly a laughing stock," Edgar cut in, a chill edge to his voice. "Everybody is wondering who Vairnruth's new favourite is."

And then I knew what had angered him. Not my behaviour, nor the way I had endangered my reputation, but the fact that Lord Vairnruth had singled me out, danced with me in front of everybody.

"You must take care," Charlotte warned. "People will talk."

"It was the two of you who brought me here," I snapped.

"I had not known you would be so eager to show yourself up." My sister gave me an exasperated look. "But perhaps I ought to have predicted it. You do not live in the real world, Emma, that much is clear. At least here nobody is sure who you are. Try to avoid exhibiting yourself any further."

With that, she swept away to rejoin Francis and their

friends. Edgar remained by my side, and together we sipped our punch in silence.

"Do you think me such an embarrassment?" I asked, at last.

Edgar sighed and looked at his feet. "You weren't to know what Lady Louisa had in mind."

"I don't understand why she did it," I lied, not daring to admit my own part in what had happened.

"It is what they do, Emma." When he caught my eye, I saw a deep sadness there. A weariness. "We are all but games to them. Something to be picked up and put down when it suits them." His gaze roved the room until he found Vairnruth, shining like the sun in the midst of a crowd of admirers. "You are new to them, and that makes you interesting. They like your innocence, your naïveté. They will make you love them, turn you into their slave, and then they will throw you away like a discarded toy. Many a woman has had her reputation left in tatters by them. Many a man has had his heart broken."

"Then why ..." I whispered. "Why bring me here at all?"

Edgar swallowed. "I had to see him. I had to. I'm sorry."

I could hear the ache in his voice, but at that moment, I could not bring myself to care.

"Would you please get me some more punch?" I passed my empty cup back to him.

Edgar hesitated, silent for a moment, then nodded and turned away.

11

I must have drunk three or four glasses of punch as I stood on the edge of the dance floor. I watched Charlotte dance with Francis, then Edgar. I watched Lord Vairnruth dance with one beautiful young lady after another, each of them gazing at him as though they could hardly believe their luck. I watched Louisa, now red-faced and giggly, dart between men like a butterfly, flirting, occasionally casting dark glances at her brother that I could not understand. Once or twice, Edgar tried to persuade me to dance, but I shook my head, staying as still as though my feet were rooted to the floor. I was afraid to do anything that would draw further attention to myself.

It seemed as I stood there that the night grew warmer and warmer, and the crush of bodies in the marquee grew increasingly dense. I fanned and fanned myself, but still sweat beaded at my hairline and slid down my chest, pooling in my cleavage. The punch was sweet and refreshing, but after a while I grew dizzy, struggling to focus on the dancers. They whirled around me, the ladies' dresses sharp slices of colour cutting through the haze of faces and masks. The candles twinkled like so many eyes. Unable to stand the heat any longer, I took a step towards the exit and stopped abruptly as the room lurched around me. My stomach flipped over; suddenly I felt terribly sick.

I hurried out beneath a garland of flowers, the cool night air hitting me like a slap in the face. For a moment, I leaned against a tree, grateful for the feel of the solid bark beneath my fingers. A few long breaths served to control my nausea, and then I decided to return to the house. Bed seemed the best place for me—bed, and the oblivion of sleep, to forget the strangeness of the night just gone.

I stumbled along the uneven dirt path, following the glow of the lanterns, and it took me some time to realise I was going the wrong way. I looked back to discover I had left the marquee from the wrong exit, and that I was walking through the woods around the edge of the house. However, I knew the route would eventually circle me back to the lawn, and from there I could easily find my way up to the Abbey. Besides, the night air was refreshing, and each step calmed my light-headedness. I was sure I would soon feel the better for it.

The lights in the tree canopy twinkled above me like stars, and for a while I wandered happily, wrapped in the pleasant warmth of intoxication. It had been a strange and confusing visit, but in a couple of days I would return home, taking with me memories of having met my idol, talked with him, even danced with him. Perhaps that would have to be enough. My seduction plan now felt foolish and ridiculous: who was I to think I could compete with all the beautiful women at the party? Not to mention all the girls Lord Vairnruth had bedded before? What would he want with the likes of me, sheltered and inexperienced as I was? No, I ought to be content with what I had, and look forward to a future with Edgar.

But my soul recoiled at the thought. Edgar was a good man, a sweet one, but he would never give me what I craved; what my body was longing for. I recalled Louisa's lips on mine, and my skin tingled with desire. How could I leave this enchanted place without tasting the fruits that had been laid out for my taking?

As I walked deeper into the woods, I began to suspect I was not alone. I had assumed the lanterns were merely there to provide decoration from a distance; it had not occurred to me that the path was lit up for a reason, but now I realised others had ventured down it before me. I noticed soft, murmuring voices, the sound of rustling amongst the leaves. Sighs. Moans.

Suddenly frightened at the thought of what I might be heading into, I told myself I ought to turn back. But my feet walked on despite my better judgement, and I rounded a corner to see two figures pressed against a tree, entangled in an embrace. I caught a glimpse of pale flesh beneath the moonlight, heard a female voice gasp with delight.

I should have moved, and yet I stood rooted to the spot, taking in the man's bare buttocks and the woman's exposed bosom. He gripped her waist, thrusting his hips faster as her cries rose in volume. I couldn't understand what I was seeing —I had no idea that women could experience such pleasure. But heat spread between my legs, the ache growing the longer I watched. I wanted to feel what she was feeling.

My desire was so strong it frightened me. I picked up my skirts and hurried through the undergrowth, wondering what on Earth had possessed me to wander so far from the party. I cursed myself for my thoughtlessness—hadn't my reputation been marred already? What would Edgar and Charlotte think of me now, when they searched the party and found me missing? They could not be wholly ignorant as to what went on here, in the shadows beneath the cover of the leaves. This place had been *meant* to provide hiding spots away from prying eyes. *That* was why the lanterns were here.

I burst out of the woodland and found myself at the edge of the lake. The sight of its placid surface, brushed to a mirror-like shine beneath the moonlight, was a relief. And above it, not far away, towered the spires of the Abbey, its windows lit up invitingly. I would catch my breath for a moment, I decided, and then I would head straight up to my room and summon Sarah to bring me a calming cup of tea for a night-cap. No-one need ever know I had been anywhere other than my own bed.

Looking down into the still water, I gazed at my own reflection. My face was moon-pale, my dark hair looked almost white in the silvery light.

"Ondine at the edge of the Moon Lake."

My heart jumped. I turned to find Lord Vairnruth watching me from between the trees.

"I'm sorry," he said, coming forward with his palms raised as if to prove he was no threat. "I didn't mean to startle you. I saw you leave the party, and I was concerned you might be unwell."

"I was." My breath was still short from my haste to escape the woods. "But the fresh air has done much to improve matters."

"I'm glad." Vairnruth stood beside me, facing the lake. I searched my mind for something to say.

"Did this ... was this lake the inspiration for the Moon Lake?"

"This? No. The Moon Lake is a real place in the Bavarian Alps. I travelled there a few years ago."

I recalled the writings I had found on his Lordship's desk the previous morning. "Is that where you learned of the legend?"

But Vairnruth didn't answer. Instead, he said, "Tell me, Miss Crawford, do you ever wonder if this is all there is?"

"What?"

"This!" Vairnruth made a sweeping gesture that seemed to encompass the house, the lake, and the marquee beyond it.

"Everything. There must be more to life than this, don't you think?"

I couldn't fathom what he was asking me. He must have been one of the richest men in England, a rare talent, famous and revered by men and women alike. And yet he was discontent?

"Surely you have everything you could possibly want?" I said. "I'm afraid I don't understand."

Vairnruth's dark eyes glinted with the light of the stars above us. "Magic," he said. "Love. Romance. Beauty! *Something*. Don't you understand what I mean? Isn't that why you came here?"

This was the perfect opportunity to go through with my campaign to seduce him, but now, suddenly alone with a man considerably older and more experienced than I, my courage failed me.

"I really ought to go back and find Edgar," I said. "He will be wondering where I am. Please excuse me."

I bowed my head and turned away, but Vairnruth spoke again. "She's real, you know."

Puzzled, I looked back. "Who is?"

A strange smile flitted across his face. "Ondine. The story is more than a myth. She lives, she exists. And I have seen her."

I stared at him, unsure if he was teasing me. "You have seen Ondine? The water nymph?"

"Sit with me," Vairnruth said. He took my hand and pulled me down to the soft sand. "I will tell you the whole story."

12

"*I* was travelling in Bavaria when I first heard of her," Vairnruth began, his warm fingers still curled around mine. His body was turned towards me, and there was a light in his eyes I had not seen before: a spark of intensity that had been lacking during my stay so far. "I stayed a night in a village on the border between Germany and Switzerland. The inn was small but friendly, and I spent the evening drinking with the locals. Many of them had fascinating stories to tell—old folklore, fairy tales, strange histories—but there was one that arrested my attention so completely that I could not stop thinking about it afterwards."

"The story of Ondine," I said.

Vairnruth nodded. "It was towards the end of the night. The fire was burning low and many of the locals had already departed for home, when finally an old man who'd listened to the conversation in silence began to speak. In a low voice, somewhat mocked by the others, he told me of a time he'd wandered too far in the forest and stumbled upon a body of water he called the Moon Lake, where he'd found a beautiful woman living in the water. The way he spoke of her fired my imagination. She was exquisite, he said, but also formidable. Unearthly. Never had he encountered such perfection and power. He was entranced. So entranced, that he was within moments of giving up his soul—and indeed, his life—to her. Only the timely intervention of his friends saved him. Worried, they had gone in search of him, and managed to track him down just in time to draw him away from the water nymph's clutches. Her fury, he said, was terrible to behold. In her anger she caused all the water of the lake to rise up and come crashing down upon them all in a tidal wave, almost drowning them as it chased them down the mountainside. They were lucky to survive.

"After I left the inn, I couldn't get the story out of my head. I had to find her. I spent weeks researching, talking to locals, putting together a map of where she might be found. And then I set off early in the morning, on my journey to the Moon Lake."

"And did you find it?" I asked. I was trying to maintain a degree of healthy scepticism, but there by the lake, listening to a story told by the great Lord Vairnruth himself, I was captivated.

"I did." Vairnruth's eyes shone in the darkness. "Picture it, my dear Miss Crawford. A lake, placid and serene, much like this one, lit by the moonlight—for it was night by the time I reached my destination. I set up my camp, but I did not sleep. Instead I waited, watching the water, hoping for a glimpse of her. She did not disappoint."

"Then you saw her?"

He shifted a little closer to me, so that our bodies were almost touching, and I held my breath as I listened to the next part of his tale.

"At first it was just a glimpse," he told me. "A pale limb in the water, and a splash as she darted back below the surface. I watched and waited, my heart in my mouth as she teased me, showing herself a little more each time. And then she rose fully from the lake, water cascading down her naked form."

I dropped his hand, and he gave me a mischievous smile. "Have I scandalised you, Miss Crawford? I am sorry. But the nymph is not human, you know. She doesn't look quite like an ordinary girl. Her skin is covered with silvery scales, like a fish, and her hair and eyes are perfectly white. I suppose she has no need for pigmentation, living as she does mostly underwater."

"I suppose," I agreed softly, feeling that I ought to make my excuses and return to the house. But, as if he sensed my intention to leave, Lord Vairnruth took my hand again.

"Stay," he said, running his thumb over my skin, "and I shall tell you what happened next."

I could not move, not while he was touching me. The fire in the base of my stomach kindled again.

"She came to me," he said, inching even closer, slipping an arm around my waist. "She did not speak. As I stared, dumfounded, she straddled me where I sat, there on the shore, and kissed me."

As he said those words, I turned to face him, and found our noses almost touching. My mind awash with nerves and confusion, I almost flinched away, but he held me tight.

"Don't imagine me a fool, Miss Crawford. You dressed up like this on purpose to tempt me," he said. His breath smelled of sweet fruit punch, but coming off his skin and hair was a scent far more masculine and primal—sweat and riding leathers and cigar smoke. It hooked me like a claw in my heart, breaking me open, spilling out curiosity and longing.

And then his lips were on mine. I had never been kissed before—not by a man—and I stiffened at first. But as the kiss grew deeper, I began to relax, and leaned into him, tasting his sweetness as he slipped his tongue into my mouth.

Gently, he pulled me on top of him, so that I sat with my legs either side of his just as the nymph must have, and I felt his manhood swelling between my thighs. Panicked, I broke away from the kiss, but he held me firm, pulling me back.

"All I want," he murmured, "is to relive that night." He kissed me again, running his hands over my breasts, slipping one beneath the thin fabric of my dress and squeezing my nipple until I cried out.

"That night was bliss," he groaned, moving his hands around to grip my buttocks. "And all since has been torture."

My body relaxed against him, knowing what to do despite the fact that my mind was all confusion. I rocked my hips against his, heat growing between my legs. Perhaps it was the intoxicating effect of all the punch, but I found I no longer cared about getting away. I only wanted to be in this moment, here, now, with this heavenly feeling building within me. Vairnruth kissed me again, and I pictured the woman I had seen rutting in the woods, her cries of ecstasy. I wanted that for myself. I wanted—I wanted—

"Emma? Emma?"

Charlotte's voice jolted me back to reality. I leapt out of Vairnruth's embrace. My sister was approaching from the woods, looking for me, but thankfully she didn't seem to have spotted me yet. Without a backward glance at his Lordship, I ran in the opposite direction, fleeing round the edge of the lake and straight across the lawn, back to the house.

I headed straight for my chambers, hoping that in the morning I would be able to convince Charlotte I had simply left the party early and gone to bed. But my mind was in disarray, and I lay awake for a long while, unable to still my whirling thoughts. It was so late by the time I fell asleep that the dawn sun was already breaking through the clouds. I tossed and turned fitfully, tangled in my sheets, my skin damp with the warmth of the summer night.

I let the Faerie King steal me away to his realm, where all was a whirl of excess and pleasure. As the king's consort, every desire I could name—and even a few I could not—were granted to me. Men and women, human and fae—all were presented for my taking, and I spent infinite days and nights in a state of delirious bliss.

Only one woman was forbidden to me: the king's sister. But I was wilful, so naturally that made me want her all the more. The most beautiful of all the fae, with a body sensuously curved and lips like rose petals, the princess stayed aloof from the others like a bird of paradise trapped in a cage. But I longed for her, this forbidden fruit, and nothing else would sate my desires. I grew jaded and languorous, tired of the constant rivalry around me. I craved respite from my luxurious prison, and so one night, in defiance of her brother's orders, I snuck into the bedchamber of the fae queen.

She sat reclined against silken pillows, clad in the sheerest of gowns that clung to her figure, leaving little to the imagination. Her golden hair tumbled around her shoulders. She looked perfect, but there was a sadness in her dark eyes.

"I wondered when you would come," she said.

"You're not surprised?"

The princess shook her head. "Everyone does, eventually. My brother's test is cruel." She lifted a hand, reaching for me, and I noticed a golden shimmer on her ivory skin. "He put a glamour on me, to make me irresistible. The same one he uses himself—the one that made you fall for him in the first place."

I paused, my eyes on her outstretched fingers. It seemed she was beckoning me to join her and trying to push me away, all at once. My longing was strong, but so was my hesitation, now that I realised I had been enchanted from the start.

"If you touch me, he will curse you."

It was a warning, spoken like an invitation. She was an illusion constructed on purpose to tempt me, to make me break my promise. I saw my own demise in her eyes and knew she had seen it all before.

But—lord! I wanted her. How could I walk away? I told myself that if I would be doomed for this transgression, I would at least partake of the forbidden fruit as fully as I could.

We made love through the night, but in the early morning, the king discovered us. He affected a jealous fury, yet I sensed enjoyment behind his rage. It was clear he got pleasure from his trick—and from its punishment.

Tearing my soul from my body, he sent me back to Earth and condemned me to live in the Moon Lake for eternity. I became bound to the water, able to feel through it, to sense its power, its reach—but unable to leave my mountaintop prison. My soulless state made me hungry, and whenever a rare traveller passed my way, I seduced him and claimed his soul for my own. But nothing was enough. Nothing could release me from the Faerie's spell. I had exchanged one cage for another.

13

When I woke the next morning, it was with a pounding headache and a stomach that felt as though it were filled with lead. I lay very still until Sarah entered, carrying a steaming cup of cocoa.

"Are you quite well, miss?" she asked.

I forced myself to sit up and my head swam. Gingerly, I accepted the cocoa and held it without taking a sip.

"I'll be fine in a moment," I said, hoping it was true. Sarah bustled around the room, tidying up my discarded dress from the night before, which she folded and placed on a chair.

"And how was the ball, miss? If you don't mind my asking?"

"It was ..." Disconnected images raced through my mind, hazy and indistinct. The marquee, with the ice peacock dripping in its centre. Vairnruth in his golden mask. The whirl of the dancers. The couple in the woods. My own reflection in the mirrored surface of the lake, looking entirely unlike myself. "It was entertaining."

Sarah gave me a sidelong glance, clearly unsatisfied by my response, but said no more. Once I felt a little better, she helped me dress, and I headed out of my room, intending to go downstairs for breakfast. I had not taken two steps, though, when a maid hurried up the corridor towards me.

"Miss Crawford." She bobbed a curtsey. "Her Ladyship sent me to fetch you. She thought you might like to take a quiet breakfast in her private parlour."

I hesitated, but as much as I didn't relish the thought of encountering Louisa, I was even less desirous to sit down in the breakfast room with everybody else. What if Vairnruth joined us? How could I possibly look him in the eye? So I nodded, and the maid escorted me to Louisa's room.

Louisa lay on a couch with the curtains drawn, still in her dressing gown. A tray of food had been placed before her, still untouched. She opened her eyes when I entered, but did not deign to move.

"Oh, Miss Crawford, I feel dreadful. You can't conceive of how I suffer. My head aches so."

I sat down opposite her. "Eat a little breakfast. Perhaps it will help."

Louisa pushed herself up to sit, making a great deal of drama about how ill she felt. I poured two cups of tea and passed one across the table.

"You are angry with me," she said, after taking a sip. "You didn't speak to me for the whole party, and when I looked for you, you were nowhere to be found."

"You surprised me. I didn't know how to react."

Louisa fixed me with a sly look over the rim of her teacup. "But you enjoyed it, didn't you? A little. Admit it."

I didn't answer. I didn't know *how* to answer. What did it matter whether I enjoyed it, when it had meant nothing to her? The question was as cruel as her behaviour had been.

"My reputation ..." I began, just as Louisa said, "I saw you by the lake with my brother, later on." Then, catching what

I'd said, she added with a sneer, "You didn't seem terribly concerned about your *reputation* then."

My face grew hot. How much had she seen? I put my teacup down. "Perhaps I ought to take breakfast with the others after all."

"My my, Miss Crawford, do not get all offended. Stay. Let us talk it through. Perhaps you'll find I am not such a poor substitute for my brother, after all."

She shifted over to sit beside me. The sofa was small, and our thighs almost touched. As she faced me, her gown fell open a little, revealing a swathe of white skin above her nightdress. I caught the same peach blossom scent of her perfume that I'd noticed the night before, and it jolted me straight back to the moment when she'd kissed me. I could almost feel her lips upon mine again.

"Emma." She put a hand on my knee, and I flinched. "I could tell the moment I saw you that you were not one of *them*."

"One of who?" *I ought to leave. I must leave.*

"How can I explain?" Louisa's hand traced its way up my thigh, and I tensed. "There are many in this world who care for *reputation* above all else. *You* are not one of them. You have more imagination than that, I feel sure."

As she spoke, she leaned closer, and her fingers neared the top of my thigh. I held my breath, knowing that I ought to leap up and leave the room, yet unable to move a muscle.

"Stay with me, Emma," Louisa whispered in my ear. Her breath was hot on my neck.

I looked straight ahead, my heart pounding. "Stay?"

"Stay here. Live with us. There's a place for you here. You don't need to go home."

"But Edgar ..."

"What did you care for Edgar yesterday, when you were desperate to seduce my brother? You don't belong with him, and you know it." She cupped my chin in her hand, making me face her, running her thumb over my lips, fixing me with her pretty, dark-eyed gaze. And I didn't move.

"I ... my sister will never agree to it."

"I'm sure you'll find a way. If you want it enough."

I felt like Ondine, on the cusp of leaving behind her mortal life and stepping into Faerie, breathless with the possibility of all the forbidden fruits laid out in front of me. And then Louisa kissed me again, and this time it was no show. There was no audience. It was real, and left me tingling from my head to my toes.

As she clutched me close, I became acutely aware of the softness of her body pressing against mine. My heart hammered, and despite the little voice inside my head telling me that this was wrong, unnatural, I relaxed into her kiss—even dared to move a hand to her waist, testing what would happen if I responded in kind.

Louisa moved her lips to my neck, pushing my hair aside in order to kiss her way down to my shoulder, only stopping when she reached the collar of my dress. Her hand still lay on my thigh, and I feared the heat of her touch would burn right through the muslin separating her skin from mine.

Maybe I didn't fear it. Maybe I wished it would.

"There, now," she murmured, pulling away. "Perhaps that will help convince you."

She got up, and I watched in stunned silence as she went to her dressing table, sitting down to brush her hair and powder her face as though nothing had happened. After a moment, she looked back at me, and I realised that I'd been staring at her.

"There's no need to look so alarmed," she laughed. "Oh, my dearest. What a time you will have, married to Edgar." She turned back to her powder. "I suppose your *reputation* will remain intact, though. Along with other things."

A maelstrom of emotions swirled inside my breast, confusion and hurt battling with the urge to run to her side and beg her to kiss me again. She was so beautiful, so cruel. Just like her brother. I wanted to cry. Instead, I stood on shaking legs.

"Please excuse me, your ladyship," I managed, and rushed out of the room.

14

I returned to my room, closed the door behind me and stood with my back pressed to it, breathing heavily. We were due to depart the following morning, and I hastened to pack my case, telling myself that it was for the best that I leave. This was not the place for me; these were not my people. Charlotte had been right, and so had Edgar. I did not want to become a just another victim of their sordid games. But when I finally went to join the others in the parlour later that morning, I found only Lord Vairnruth waiting for me.

He was pacing in front of the window and turned to me as I entered. I hesitated, my hand still on the doorknob, then summoned all my courage and approached him.

"My Lord, we should talk," I said.

"Talk?" He raised his eyebrows. "About how you ran away from me last night? You are a true temptress, Miss Crawford."

He took a step towards me, and I backed away. I wasn't sure if it was him I didn't trust, or myself. "Where are the others?"

"Out riding. Well, aside from Lolly, who I suppose is still asleep. You haven't seen her this morning, have you?"

Something in his tone made me suspect he knew about my breakfast with Louisa, but I shook my head anyway.

"So you see," he said, "we are alone, and may *talk* as much as we please."

I do not think my heart could have beat any faster if I had been a mouse, and he a cat standing over me with his teeth bared. I was about to be devoured... and to my surprise, I liked it.

But then he turned to face the window, looking out at the lake.

"I have a question for you, Miss Crawford, but I fear you will not think me serious on such a short acquaintance as we have had."

"A question?" I stepped up behind him, close enough to touch his arm. "About what?"

He looked at me then, and there was a glint in his eye that disturbed me. A look of naked hunger that he quickly blinked away, replacing it with a smile that appeared bland and fake.

"You and I have talked little," he said, "but talking is only one form of communication. I sense we understand one another on some deeper level, wouldn't you agree?"

I opened my mouth to speak, but had no idea what to say. His words echoed the feelings of my own heart. Could it be true? Was it possible he really felt the same? I felt a pang of guilt when I considered that I had just kissed his sister—but who did I think I was betraying? Him, or her?

"You say little," he said, fixing his gaze on mine. "But I know you feel much, in here." And he placed his hand on my bosom, over my racing heart. "What I ask is that you marry me. Soon. Tonight."

My heart stalled. Perhaps on some level I had been expecting this from the moment he'd told me he had a question, but still I was thrown into confusion, unable to answer.

"What about Edgar?" I managed to stammer.

The hungry look flared behind Vainruth's eyes again, and with it a spark of anger—quickly extinguished.

"Edgar is only using you," he said. "You must surely be aware of that. Think of what I can give you. This place, this life. What does he have to offer that can possibly compare?"

He was right, of course, on all points. And Edgar would hardly miss me. I was nothing but a convenience to him. This was the opportunity I had been waiting for—the opportunity to stay. To be close to Vairnruth—*and Louisa*, a small voice whispered in my ear—for the rest of my life.

Yet still I hesitated.

Vairnruth's expression softened. He brushed a hair away from my face with a gentle gesture. "Let me convince you."

He kissed me, pulling me tight against his chest, his grip firm around my waist. His scent of riding leathers and cigar smoke filled my nostrils as he manoeuvred me against the wall, pinning me there with his knee between my legs.

I squirmed against his leg, enjoying the pressure, wanting more. He picked me up as if I were nothing and carried me over to the sofa where he lay me down, his hands exploring beneath my dress. This time, I was ready, and I let myself relax into his touch. I closed my eyes, thinking of the Faerie King from my dreams. I would not resist, I decided. I would worship him, the way Ondine had worshipped her prince, and perhaps he would take me, too, to somewhere better than this mundane world.

Hitching my dress up around my waist, he slid a hand up the inside of my thigh, and my legs opened of their own accord, inviting him to reach higher. I thought of the couple in the trees—the woman's moans growing louder. I thought of Louisa's teasing. Half-crazed with how badly I wanted to be touched, I raised my hips, and Vainruth caught my eye.

"Poor Emma," he murmured with a smile. "Did my sister not satisfy you?"

He ran his thumb over my bud and I gasped. Then he pressed harder, rubbing in slow circles, and while I mewled with delight he took hold of my hand and pressed it to his manhood, entreating me to stroke the bulge in his breeches.

Vairnruth withdrew his hand from between my legs, and I whimpered with the loss. He stood, and for a moment I saw myself as he must have done, sprawled on the sofa with my legs wide, completely exposed, like a common whore. Heat rushed to my cheeks. But I was soon distracted by the sight of him unbuttoning his breeches, and by the time he held his erect member in his hand, pumping it a little up and down, I wanted nothing but to reach for him, to draw him closer.

When he entered me, I was slick and wet enough to make it easy. I gasped as he filled me, my mind reeling with all the new sensations. It felt good—no, it felt *heavenly*. How could something so blissful possibly be sin?

He ground against me, and I wrapped my legs around his waist, drawing him even deeper inside. Soon, we were moving in unison, pleasure coiling tight in my belly until I thought I would explode. I cried out, my body clenching around him. Waves of ecstasy rippled through me. Vairnruth let out a moan and slumped against me, spent.

And then I saw her.

A pale figure watched us through the window, one webbed hand pressed up against the glass. Water poured down her naked body, and when she opened her mouth in a ghastly smile, her teeth were sharp as knives.

15

I startled and scrambled out from under Lord Vairnruth, but by the time I looked again the strange figure at the window had vanished.

"What's the matter?" Vairnruth sat back on the couch, lacing up his breeches. "Did I hurt you?"

"No, I saw—" The words caught in my throat. Surely he would think I had lost my mind. "Nothing. It's nothing."

He regarded me complacently, his manner far more relaxed than it had previously been. "You are quite unique, Miss Crawford. Or may I call you Emma now? We do know each other intimately, after all."

"If you wish." I hastily rearranged my dress, fearing that Louisa might walk in on us at any moment. I didn't want her to know what had just happened. I felt strangely empty, and a little guilty, as though some other girl had lain on that couch with Lord Vairnruth, and I had merely watched. *What now?* I wondered, as Vairnruth got up to open the drinks cabinet. In a few short minutes I had become a fallen woman. *A whore*, a little voice said inside my mind—a little voice that sounded a lot like Charlotte. Vairnruth had asked me to marry him, and it seemed I had made my choice. My father would never forgive me. No other man would ever have me. I would have to say yes.

"Brandy?" Vairnruth poured two glasses and passed one to me. I was shaking a little, and the sharp alcohol helped to calm my nerves. My whole world had changed, while for him it was just another day.

He sat back down on the couch, hooking one ankle over the other knee, quite at his ease. "Have you considered your answer yet?"

I looked at him, and realised I was seeing a stranger. I thought I had known him through his writing, but I was wrong. Something about the look in his eyes chilled me. Behind his veneer of charm there was nothing but the hunger I had seen before. No life, no warmth. He seemed ... empty.

The longer I hesitated, the darker his expression grew, and I realised I was afraid. Afraid of what might happen if I said no.

Afraid of what might happen if I said yes.

"Think about it," he said at last, speaking slowly as though it took tremendous patience to form the words. "But it must be tonight, by the lake." A thought seemed to strike him, and his mouth curved into a mirthless smile. "Wear your Ondine costume."

And then he left me.

I tried to finish my brandy, but the taste made me sick, and I put the half-full glass aside. I felt unsettled, as though I were treading on uneven ground, and I decided some fresh air might help.

I went outside and headed towards the lake. I couldn't stop thinking about the strange figure I had seen outside the window, connecting it to the glimpse I'd had of a face not my own in the water. The more I considered it, the more I was sure I had not seen my own reflection, but something else.

Combined with the papers I'd glimpsed in Vairnruth's library, his frequent references to a mystery woman, and his insistence that the water nymph was real, I had a strong suspicion about what he was really keeping here in the lake.

Approaching the edge of the lake, I slipped off my shoes and hiked my skirt up to just above my ankles, so that I might dip my toes in the water. The day was warm, and the coolness of the lake was a welcome relief. I stood for a while enjoying the sensation, and gazing at the mirror-like surface of the water, which reflected the blue sky above. There was nothing to be seen below.

"Ondine?" I said, in little more than a whisper. "Ondine, are you here?"

Nothing answered me. The lake remained utterly still, and in that moment I realised how badly I had wanted to believe in her. In some kind of magic beyond the ordinary. But perhaps I ought to be glad at her non-appearance. At the window, she had looked angry, and it was possible she meant me harm.

Yet curiosity drove me on. I hitched my dress up further and waded a few more steps into the lake. The Abbey, though visible, was distant. No-one was watching. I swept a palm across the lake's surface and watched my own reflection ripple in the water, searching for the pale girl I'd seen the night before. But my face looked as dull and ordinary as ever.

"Ondine, I'm sorry. I didn't mean to anger you. I need your help ..."

It occurred to me that the lake was vast, and if she were lurking at the other side or sleeping somewhere in the depths, she might not hear me. Hastily, fearing I might change my mind at any moment, I unlaced my dress and pulled it off over my head, tossing it to the sand. Then, I fumbled with my tight corset, freeing myself from its bonds so that I stood there in nothing but my thin linen shift. Already I felt better, my breath freer, my limbs released from the weight of the dress.

I waded into the water, deeper and deeper with every step. My shift billowed up around my waist, floating on the surface of the water. Realising it was useless for modesty, I discarded it and plunged into the lake fully naked. I would swim its circumference once, I told myself, just to be sure the water nymph was not here, and then I would return to the shore before anyone saw me.

The sensation of the water on my skin was blissful, and I lingered longer than I ought, swimming first round the edge of the lake as planned, and then heading for its dark centre. As I swam, I imagined where this water had once been; how far it must have travelled before settling in this very lake. Its memory leaked into me through my skin. I saw snow falling on mountain peaks; glaciers, frozen for millennia; clear alpine streams joining rushing rivers that grew to a majestic size before cutting a swathe through bustling cities. I saw wild seas buffeted by storms; deep, unfathomable oceans teeming with life. I saw the water's power, the way it shaped entire landscapes, destroying whole communities with a single wave. And then I saw myself, as if from above. One small, lone figure floating in the centre of it all. Insignificant. Isolated.

Trapped.

I could marry Vairnruth. I could stay forever, but what would I be doing other than swapping one prison for another? Louisa had told me herself that her brother never permitted her to leave this place. Wouldn't it be the same for me? I could live forever in Faerie, with pleasures untold at my fingertips, but it would mean I could never belong to society again. Or ... It occurred to me that no one but Vairnruth and I need ever know what I had done. I could stave off my return to reality for a few more days, and then go home to marry Edgar. It was difficult to tell which option was worse. I wanted neither of them. The water was showing me the size of the world I would never be a part of, and my chest ached with grief at the thought.

As I stared into the deep blue of the sky, a feathery touch on my ankle jolted me out of my thoughts. A fish, I assumed, but as I turned onto my front to swim back to shore, I spotted something silvery moving just beneath the surface. Treading water, I watched the shape flit around me, vanishing into the darkness on occasion, only to reappear elsewhere in the lake. Suddenly, dry land felt a long way away.

Intending to get away, I pushed myself forward—and felt the touch on my ankle again, tighter this time. I tried to swim, but it held me fast, its grip curling like icy fingers around my leg. The harder I battled to escape, the more it tugged at me, pulling me down until I was thrashing on the surface, desperately trying to keep my head above water.

All my efforts were in vain. The *thing*—whatever it was— tugged at me and I found myself helplessly dragged into the depths of the lake, the scream that had been in my mouth silenced as my lungs filled with water.

I was drowning. There was nothing I could do. The water was black and cold, the light of the sun already unreachable above me. It was too late even to panic, and so I grew strangely calm, numb to the cries of my body for desperately needed air.

The grip on my leg loosened, and the silver shape flitted around me once more, coming to a stop directly in front of my face. I had time to register pale features that looked vaguely female, and white hair that drifted around her face like seaweed, before her lips were on mine, and suddenly I could breathe again.

I clung to her, wanting to weep from relief. When she released me, I was no longer drowning. Somehow, she had given me the ability to survive in the depths of the lake. I stared at her, a vision with her opalescent eyes and flat, slitted nose.

She placed her webbed hand on my arm, and I felt, rather than heard, her voice.

I will help you ... if you free me.

After she spoke, the water nymph released me and disappeared into the darkness. Kicking hard, I returned to the surface without difficulty, gasping as I broke through the skin of the water. I swam for shore and hastily pulled on my dress. As I hurried around the lake's edge, I examined its still surface for any evidence of the creature I had just met. But she was nowhere to be seen. Had I imagined her? Had she, in fact, been a hallucination brought on by the terror of my near-death experience?

I will help you ... if you free me.

Her voice echoed in my mind, becoming a mantra. *Free me. Free me.*

16

On returning to the house, I followed the twinkling sound of the pianoforte to the parlour, where I found Louisa alone. She stopped playing when she noticed me enter, and I was struck hard by her beauty, gripped by a sudden longing to get as close to her as I could. Perhaps I had been unfair to her. She'd been so happy to have me here, so happy to have a friend—an equal. We could be friends, couldn't we?

Perhaps we could be something more.

The memory of her kiss rushed into my mind. I wanted to do it again; to do more than just kiss. I wanted to see her pretty eyes cloud with pleasure and hear a sigh of delight escape her lips.

But first, I had to talk to her about what had just happened to me.

"Did you make a decision, dear Emma?" Rising from the pianoforte, she approached me and slipped her arms around my waist. For a shocked moment I thought she knew about her brother's proposal.

"A decision?"

"About whether to stay!" She scrutinised my face. "You look paler than usual. And you're soaking wet! Are you cold?" She pulled me closer, our bodies crushed together. "Let me warm you up."

Her lips were on mine before I could protest, and for a moment I let myself drown in her kiss, intoxicated by her sweet taste. I was exhausted by my morning's escapades, yet the fire in the base of my stomach was easily lit, and it took all my self-control to pull away and focus once more on what I wanted to say to her.

"Wait," I said, stopping her as her fingers played with the shoulder of my dress. "I need to ask you something. It's important."

"Oh?" She raised her eyebrows.

I led her over to the couch, where we sat down together. I tried not to think about what I had done with her brother in this very spot, mere hours ago. I felt sure she would be angry if she knew.

"Please don't think I've taken leave of my senses," I began. "But I need to know—is your brother keeping something in the lake?"

Louisa's brows knit together in thought, and I realised with relief that she was taking me seriously. "I suppose you're not referring to the fish."

I shook my head. "On the night I arrived, I saw a crate being delivered and taken down to the lake. And today ..."

"Today ...?"

"I saw her. The water nymph." My words came out in a rush. "I think she's living in the lake. I think ... I think Lord Vairnruth is keeping her prisoner."

"The water nymph?" Louisa repeated slowly, her eyes fixed on mine. "Whatever do you mean?"

"The nymph. From your brother's story. Ondine." I frowned. "You think I'm mad."

"No, Emma, I'm trying to understand."

I sighed. "The truth is, I'm afraid perhaps I *am* mad. Ever since I came here, everything feels strange. Unreal. But his Lordship told me she existed. He found her in a lake in the Alps, and I'm beginning to suspect he found a way to bring her back here. Are you saying you know nothing about it?"

"Nothing. But listen—I believe you." She squeezed my hand. "If you say you saw something, I'm sure you did. The truth is, ever since Augustus returned from Germany he has been changed, somehow. He was always mercurial, prone to fits of depression. Edgar can confirm that. But now ... Now there's a coldness to him that wasn't there before. He's darker, more controlling, more jealous. It's as if he's lost something, and in its place came this obsession with *her*—with the water nymph." Her eyes misted with sadness. "He's not the brother I knew. Not anymore."

"When you dressed me up as Ondine ..."

"I was trying to get a reaction out of him. Ever since I was a child, my whole world has revolved around Augustus. He used to feel the same about me. He was a doting brother, always looking out for me. But since he came back from Europe and wrote that dratted water nymph poem, it's as though I'm no more than another possession of his. I've done everything I could think of to please him, to get him to notice me, but nothing is good enough, because all he cares about is *her*. He's been obsessed with her, to the total exclusion of everything else—including the dratted house renovations. If he *is* somehow keeping her in the lake, well, that would make perfect sense." She sighed. "I was so furious with him. I still am. But it was wrong of me to use you the way I did. I'm sorry."

Any anger I still felt towards Louisa melted away in the face of her heartfelt apology. She had a guileless honesty that made it impossible to think badly of her.

"You are forgiven," I said, opening my arms. She slipped into my embrace easily, as though she belonged there. Her body was warm against mine. I stroked her satiny hair and kissed the top of her head.

"I think it worked, though, didn't it?" she murmured. "Your plan to seduce Augustus?"

"It did," I admitted. "Better than I could have hoped. But I'm not sure it was what I really wanted after all."

She looked up at me, her face close to mine, her eyes curious. "What is it you do want?"

There was something about the smile that played at the corners of her mouth that told me she knew exactly what was in my heart. And yet, part of me still hesitated, fearing that I was being tricked somehow. Ever since I'd arrived at Northwood Abbey, it was as though I'd sunk into some feverish dream. I no longer knew what to believe or who to trust. Yet I could not ignore the longing that surged through my body when I looked at her pink lips.

"I want this," I said, and kissed her.

The moment I did it, I knew that I was right. Holding Louisa, feeling the press of her body against mine, was like coming home. Unlike with Vairnruth, I wanted to please her out of generosity, not fear. I wanted to feel her body tremble at my touch. Our kiss deepened, and she slipped her tongue into my mouth, teasingly. Her sweet taste made me ache for more. I broke away, only to run a line of kisses down her neck, sweeping her hair aside, enjoying the velvety softness of her skin and the orange blossom scent that filled my nose.

"Let's go upstairs," she whispered.

We hurried through the house, holding hands, stopping every few steps to press against each other and kiss again. At the foot of the stairs she started to unlace my dress, and I ran my hands down her back to clutch her round buttocks. I didn't know how we would make it to her room, so desperate were we to have each other naked, but then we footsteps and ran again, laughing, up the stairs and through the door.

As Louisa closed and locked it, I finished the unlacing of my dress, and by the time she faced me I was sliding it slowly off my shoulders. I let it pool at my feet, and she approached to help me remove my corset and petticoats.

"No," I said. "I want to see you first."

Reverently, I undressed her, kissing every inch of bare skin I uncovered. Then I stepped back to take in her full figure, her creamy skin, her broad, rose-pink nipples, the blonde fuzz of hair between her legs. She was breathtaking.

"Sit," I told her, gesturing to the bed, and Louisa obeyed.

I started at her feet, gazing up at her like I were a supplicant and she, my goddess. I kissed my way up her leg, gently spreading her thighs apart when I reached them, caressing the soft skin on their insides.

"Emma." Louisa sighed my name, her hand drifting between her legs. I gently pushed it away and opened her legs wider, wanting that prize for myself. She lay back, and I delved in, inhaling her musky scent, kissing the petal-like lips of her nether regions until I found the spot that made her gasp.

She squirmed beneath me, one hand on my head, her hips arching with every lick of my tongue. I was in heaven. I felt that I could do this forever. But eventually she let out a loud cry, and her body shuddered and released. I crawled my way up her, and our lips met, our bodies mingling. I hooked a leg over her waist and she slipped a finger inside me, then another. I was slick and wet as a sea creature. As my pleasure built, I clung to her, closing my eyes, sinking into a blissful darkness. Down, down, into the depths of the water. Drowning again—

But not drowning.

Living. Breaking out from my prison.

Becoming free.

17

*A*fterwards, Louisa and I lay curled up in one another's arms for a long time, sweaty and blissful and—the feeling that surprised me most—*safe*. Here, I thought, was what I hadn't known I was looking for. Here, I belonged.

But before long, it was time to go down for dinner. Reluctantly, we unfurled ourselves from our embrace, and helped each other to dress, all shy smiles and fumbling fingers. My heart was so light I thought I might fly. As Louisa turned to head downstairs, I stopped her.

"I'll stay," I said. "Even if it means I have to marry your brother. I'll do anything. I want to stay."

Louisa looked me in the eye. I thought she would smile and hug me, but she didn't, she only looked wistful.

"I wish you could," she said. "But Emma, I can't let you exchange one prison for another. Whatever you do, do not marry Augustus. I was wrong to ask you to remain here. Not when there's a whole world out there for you."

My mood sank, my joy turning to hopelessness in a moment.

"I don't want the world. I want to be with you."

Louisa squeezed my hand, then kissed me on the cheek. "You have a good heart, dear Emma. Let that be your guide."

Blinking away a tear, I composed myself, and we headed to the dining room.

Despite the warm night, the fire blazed and the air in the room was close, almost suffocating. There were half a dozen other guests for dinner aside from myself, Charlotte, Edgar, Louisa, and Vairnruth himself.

I sat beside Edgar, and although we spoke little, I felt we were compatriots in our mutual discomfort. His eyes were, as always, fixed on his old friend, while Vairnruth's were fixed on me. I withered under the intensity of his Lordship's gaze, and looked down at my plate in order to avoid his silent questioning. *It must be tonight*, he had said. Why the hurry? He wanted something from me, but I could not figure out what.

The drink flowed freely, and I overindulged without meaning to, my wine glass topped up by ever-attentive staff the moment I took a sip. Stuffed with food and giddy from the wine, I watched as the main course was cleared away and the desserts brought out. The very sight of them made me queasy.

But there was not to be time to eat any more, even if I had wanted to. Before we could continue our feast, Vairnruth pushed his chair back violently and stood, tapping his wine glass with a spoon to get our attention. In the few hours since I had seen him last, he had undergone a most alarming transformation. His dark eyes were sunken in their sockets, ringed with purple as though he hadn't slept in weeks. His skin was bone-pale, stretched against his skull. His hands shook, and he struggled to breathe, clutching his chest as though he were drowning.

"Dearly beloved," he began, his mouth curling into a sneer. "Dearly beloved, we are gathered here today to mourn the untimely passing of one Lord Augustus Vairnruth—degenerate, pervert, worthless, untalented wretch, and vile stain on his father's good name. Alas he passed away mere hours after his thirtieth birthday, but no matter. He shall not be mourned."

He grinned, and the company around the table laughed uproariously, as though he had made some wonderful jest. Charlotte clapped her hands, beaming and red-cheeked. Louisa smiled wanly, more subdued than I had ever seen her. Only Edgar and I did not respond with merriment, and I could see that he was concerned, as I was, for his friend's health and state of mind. What had happened to him?

Free me, Ondine's voice whispered in my ear.

"You all assume I'm joking." Vairnruth said, with a wild laugh that disintegrated into a wheezing cough. For a moment I was afraid he would keel over where he stood. "What a bunch of mindless sycophants you are. Yes, go on, keep laughing! I am nothing but a spectacle to you people. Nothing but a performing seal!"

Dashing his wine glass to the floor, he climbed up onto the table, sending plates clattering.

"Augustus." Louisa's voice was a warning. "Do not make yourself absurd."

"Absurd, Lolly? You find me absurd? But I am deadly serious. Augustus Vairnruth is no more. He is dead! He is gone. His soul hath departed this mortal plane, and where it has gone, none can say. You are all here celebrating the birthday of a corpse."

By now, the general amusement had died down and the guests were looking at one another, puzzled.

"Emma." I tensed as Vairnruth turned to me, extending a hand. "My dear Emma, my wife to be. Come and join me, and we shall be married tonight."

I looked at Louisa, whose eyes were wide with alarm. She shook her head, and so I did not move. But Vairnruth was insistent.

"Join me." His voice darkened, and a look of hatred flashed in his eyes. Fearing what he might do if I refused, I let him pull me up onto the table beside him.

"Now, my pretty temptress." He placed his hands on either side of my head and ran them down my hair, in a motion that made my spine tingle. "You came into this house, all beauty and disruption, and claimed you wanted to save me." His hands came to rest on my shoulders, alarmingly close to my throat. "Now is your chance. Let us go to the lakeside and perform the ceremony immediately."

His broad grin was terrible to behold. He looked insane. My heart hammered in my chest as his hands moved to my neck.

"I will not," I whispered, darting my eyes this way and that, catching glimpses of faces—some horrified, some mirthful.

"What's that?" Vairnruth cocked his head as though he hadn't heard me, though I knew he must have.

"I said I will not." I repeated, as loudly and firmly as I could manage. By now I knew whatever he had in store for me, it could be nothing good.

"You're a whore, Emma." Charlotte's voice rang clear and true, as if it were coming from inside my own skull. "We all know it. Why don't you admit the truth?"

No sooner had she spoken than the rest of the table took up the chant: *Whore. Whore. Whore!* All but Louisa and Edgar joined in, bashing their cutlery on the table. The room whirled around me and I grew dizzy; I hardly knew what was real and what was in my mind.

"You conspired against me, didn't you?" Vairnruth went on, with a snarl. "You and my devious sister. She wants me dead, don't you Lolly? Well now, you will get your wish. She's killing me. The nymph," he took another unsteady breath, "is killing me. Is that what you wanted?"

Edgar got to his feet. "That's enough. Let Miss Crawford go."

Vairnruth laughed, his black eyes sparkling. "Why are you here, Edgar?" he demanded. "Why, after all I have done to you?"

Edgar blanched. "Done to me?"

"Poor, poor Edgar."

Vairnruth released me, and I jumped off the table out of reach as Vairnruth pulled his friend up in my stead. He wrapped a hand round the back of Edgar's neck.

"Once we were best friends. The very best. And then I spurned you, didn't I? You know why. You know how cold I was, how much of a hypocrite. It was all about reputation with me, you see. I liked to court the rumours—but I could not allow anyone to take them too seriously."

He put his face close to Edgar's, whose eyes had welled up with tears. "I have treated you ill, my dear, dear friend. And I do not care, you see? I don't feel a thing. I don't feel a damned thing!"

He shoved Edgar hard, and the taller man lost his footing, slamming down amongst the dishes. Plates and cutlery flew everywhere. The guests shrieked and jumped up from the table. Edgar blinked up at Vairnruth, dumbfounded.

"I don't feel a damned thing," Vairnruth repeated, his voice low and sinister. "I could kill you right now, in front of all these people, and I wouldn't feel a shred of remorse. My oldest friend. More than friend. Someone I could have loved, had *she* not turned my heart black as night."

"Augustus ..." Louisa's voice trembled. "What are you doing?"

"What am I doing, Lolly?" Vairnruth swiped a carving knife from the table and bore down on the still stunned Edgar. "Proving a point, that's what I'm doing."

"Augustus," Edgar begged. "This isn't you. I know you. Please ..."

"You never knew me," Vairnruth spat. "None of you ever did. Only what you wanted me to be. You loved an illusion, Edgar, you damned fool."

I never imagined he would do it, not even as he knelt above my supposed fiancé and raised the knife. Some of the guests were still chuckling, still imagining this was some kind of performance for their amusement. Edgar himself was frozen in place, his face a mask of horror. I could see in his eyes the confusion of emotions that he felt at that moment, as the person he loved most in the world—had remained devoted to for so long despite Vairnruth's lack of interest—threatened to harm him. But as the knife came down towards his throat, the hurt gave way to something else, something softer: resignation, as though he had known it would end this way all along. As though he welcomed it.

Vairnruth sliced his friend's throat as though he were carving meat for the dinner. The ladies cried out in horror, turning pale, fainting away. The gentlemen rushed forward to apprehend their host—too late, for blood was already flowing from Edgar's wound, so deep I was sure it must be mortal. As his friends dragged an unresisting Vairnruth off the table, Edgar's eyelids fluttered and he let out a terrible, gurgling gasp, struggling to breathe.

Then he fell silent.

18

A stillness descended upon the dining room. Edgar's body lay in the centre of the table, blood oozing from the wound in his throat. Vairnruth stood nearby, his shirt soaked with red, the dripping knife hanging loosely from his hand. Two gentlemen held his arms, although the measure seemed unnecessary given that Vairnruth looked disinclined to struggle or run. Indeed, for a man who had just committed the murder of his best friend, he looked remarkably calm. Emotionless.

Charlotte sat down heavily on the nearest chair, white-faced, her hands on her belly. The other guests murmured to each other, hesitant, still unsure whether this were not some elaborate practical joke; whether Edgar would not suddenly leap up from the table and take a bow and everyone would laugh heartily and pour another drink.

I, too, was willing to consider that possibility. It seemed far easier than acknowledging the fact that Edgar—*dear Edgar*, as I now found myself thinking of him—was really dead. A discussion broke out amongst the gentlemen as they considered what to do with Vairnruth. Should they lock him up? Should they report him to the local magistrate? Some were determined to defend their friend despite his actions, believing him to be unwell, while others feared that none of us were safe with such a madman in our midst. For my part, I was in such a state of panic that I struggled to accept the evidence of my own eyes. I was certain I was watching a play. A dumbshow of horror. How had I become trapped in this nightmarish place?

Only Louisa seemed to have the presence of mind to manage the situation. She stood on the other side of the room from me, a little way behind her brother, and when she caught my eye I saw a flicker of panic, dismissed in the space of a blink. Drawing herself up, she took a deep breath and, in a cold, steady voice quite unlike her usual tone, said, "It seems dinner is at an end. We shall make our way to the drawing room for drinks, ladies and gentlemen. Please follow me."

She headed for the door without another word, her back very straight and stiff. I hurried after her and touched her arm as we reached the exit.

"Louisa, please ..."

I didn't know what I was intending to say. Please tell me what's happening here? Please don't ignore the fact that Edgar is dead? But she turned to me, and my words caught in my throat when I saw her blink back tears. She forced her expression into a smile, and grasped my hand.

"It will be all right, Emma dear. You'll see."

"How can you say that?" I began, but before I could say more, a scuffle erupted behind us. Vairnruth had broken away from the gentlemen who had apprehended him and now approached me.

"Now, Miss Crawford, you see you are no longer encumbered by any fiancé." His clammy fingers wrapped around mine. "It is time we held our ceremony."

I looked around for help, but none was forthcoming. It

seemed the other guests were too stunned and frightened to intervene. Or perhaps they were simply enjoying the spectacle.

"A wedding!" Vairnruth repeated, raising our linked hands in the air.

The room lurched around me as the guests raised their glasses. "A wedding!" Their faces leered at me, strange and terrifying. They were like dogs, salivating for entertainment.

"You killed him," I cried, as Vairnruth dragged me through the door, followed by the mob. I don't know how I managed to speak, for I was so numb all over it was a miracle I could move my lips. "You killed him. I don't understand. Why? Tell me why!"

"Because I could," he replied. "Because I wanted to show you all—and *you*, especially, Miss Crawford—what I am."

"And what *are* you?"

We were in the hallway by then, and an icy breeze blew through the house, flickering the candles in their sconces.

"A monster." Vairnruth fixed me for a moment with an intense look. "You said you wanted to save me. So save me." He pulled me onwards, running out into the night. As he dragged me down the lawn, I looked back at the guests following, whooping and yelling. Louisa was at their head, hurrying to catch up, her shouts of 'Augustus!' drowned in the general hubbub. She tripped and disappeared beneath trampling feet. Screaming her name, I tried to struggle out of Vairnruth's grip, but he picked me up and threw me over his shoulder. My shouts only seemed to inflame the crowd's excitement.

Eventually we reached the lake, where Vairnruth dropped me unceremoniously onto the stony shore.

"Now, my dear," he pulled me to my feet, "we can be wed." He raised his voice, shouting over the water. "A soul for a soul, Ondine! Take hers, and return mine to me. Or give me a bride as soulless as myself."

And then I understood. In his version of the Ondine story,

the soulless Ondine had to marry a pure, faithful human in order to regain her soul. For Vainruth, I was to be that person. A sacrifice. A pure, faithful soul in exchange for his own. He would marry me, or kill me. It didn't matter which, so long as he regained the soul that had allowed him to write. That had made him famous.

He pushed me forward, and I had no choice but to stumble into the lake. A sense of calm suffused me, even as he followed me, forcing me in up to my waist. Even as he put his hands on my head and pushed me under. The water folded over me like an embrace, and I felt no fear.

Free me.

I stared into the underwater darkness, and before long I caught a glimpse of silver from the corner of my eye. She appeared before me: not the perfect, sensuous, woman-like beauty of Vairnruth's poem, but a being alien to my eyes, sleek and powerful, with slits for a nose and unnaturally large eyes. Her white hair was not hair at all, but many fine, waving fronds, like thin tentacles. Yet as she swam towards me, she began to change. Slowly, subtly, her features resolved into something more human. Her 'hair' thickened and grew darker, more like real hair. More like mine. By the time she faced me, I was astounded to find I was looking at my own reflection.

I blinked; the nymph blinked. I moved my head; the nymph moved her head. I raised my hand; the nymph raised her hand, and our palms pressed together.

"I don't understand." Although I could not speak underwater, my mouth formed the words, and she mimicked me. She looked at me intently, through my very own eyes, and—I don't know how else to explain this—I felt a rush of information flow from her to me. All at once, everything grew clear.

· · ·

Over the centuries, many men passed my way. Foolish dreamers looking for adventure. I could sense them as they approached my lake, a mixture of naive hope and hubris bringing them searching. Every one of them thought they could tame me, make me their own.

But no man can tame water. Each man I met, I tested, looking for one whose intentions were pure: who would love me enough to carry me away from the Moon Lake and then let me go. But none were willing. They saw me as a prize, a possession, something they could show off and brag about. So I kissed them, and took their souls, and left them either dead or broken, dissatisfied, unable ever to find happiness.

And Vairnruth? Foolishly, some part of me still hoped every man who came to me would turn out to be different. But this one —this one was familiar in a way I could not explain. It was only after he had made love to me by the Moon Lake that I realised why. He reminded me of the Faerie King, whom I had not seen for so many centuries. His touch awakened some remnant of sentiment within my dead heart, and when I tried to take his soul, for once his pleas for mercy did not fall on deaf ears.

He told me he loved me and I, like the innocent maiden I had once been ... I believed him. Perhaps, I hoped, he was the one who would release me from my captivity. When he returned a few weeks later with a whole group of men, he swore he would free me, and so I submitted to his capture willingly.

Foolish, foolish Ondine! They took me from the lake in a cage and subjected me to weeks of travel out of the water. Every moment was torture. I struggled to breathe, to survive above the surface. My scales grew dry, my hair dropped out. By the time we reached Northwood Abbey, I was so unlike my former self that Vairnruth looked upon me with disgust. I was delivered in the night and, on examining me in the light of day, he found that his shiny jewel, whose arrival he had so anticipated, was now nothing more than a dry, ragged, miserable shell of her former self. When I refused to return his soul, he was furious, and swore that I would remain where I was until he broke me, no matter how long it took.

But I will not be broken.

19

After absorbing all of Ondine's memories, her thoughts and feelings, I dreamed myself free. Flowing with the river, rolling with the oceans. I was everywhere, I was elemental, I was supreme. A giver of life, a part of every human and animal on the globe, running through their blood. I was manna falling from heaven on dry soil. And I was a killer, a storm, a tempest, a fearsome whip of waves on angry seas. I was not just Emma anymore—I was more, so much more. I did not belong in this lake-prison where Vairnruth, in his hubris, had trapped me.

With one great push to the surface, I rose from the lake rejuvenated and fearsome, my body thrilling with new-found power. I walked onto shore soaked to the skin. The thin fabric of my dress clung to my body, but I felt no cold, only searing anger.

Vairnruth stood on the sand, and I relished the confusion on his face. He had not expected to see me restored to my full glory. Not after trapping me here. But I too was confused, as I tried to make sense of the jumble of memories now flooding my mind. Ondine's experiences battled with Emma's for supremacy, and I feared my head would explode. The only thing that remained clear was the anger, and I clung to it, desperate for certainty amidst the maelstrom of confusion. My fists clenched with fury.

I must have been underwater for a long while. The night was over. Dawn lit the Abbey's facade with golden light, sunrise sparkling on the water. In the light of day, the guests from the party looked like mere puppets. They stood holding their half-full wine glasses, their hair and clothes in disarray, makeup smeared over their faces. What kind of spell had Vairnruth put them under, that they were so unmoved? So empty and inhuman?

I thought of Edgar, whose only crime had been to love someone who did not deserve it, and whose demise they had laughed and made merry over as if it were no more than a play for their amusement. I hated them. I hated them all.

My eye roved over the crowd until I caught sight of Louisa. From the fear writ all over her face, I realised that my appearance must have changed, and I looked down at my hands. Silver scales covered their backs, running all the way up my arms. My nails were long and brittle, coated with green algae. Glancing at my reflection in the water, I saw that my hair had paled to whiteness, and my face was changing too, my nose flattening, my eyes narrowing to slits. I smiled. It was quite a hideous sight now that my lips had all but vanished, and my teeth were sharp as a predator's.

Sensing someone approaching, I turned, whip-fast, to find Vairnruth within arm's reach. Hunger built in the pit of my stomach—a kind of hunger I had never felt before, all-consuming, infecting every part of my body with an unbearable craving. Not for food, but for souls. Human souls.

No, not just human ... In the golden light of the morning I saw him anew, lit from behind by the sunrise so that the ends of his hair glowed as if on fire. Surely there was only one who could have captured me the way he did.

It was him. The Faerie King. I was convinced of it. Only his death could break the curse he'd set upon me and set me free.

He shrank back at the sight of my face.

"Emma ..." he tried, holding up his hands as if in surrender.

But it was too late. I fell upon him, using all my strength to push him onto the wet sand. Pinning him down, I clamped my legs either side of his torso. He put his hands on my shoulders, struggling to hold me off, but I was a tangle of lust and wanting, needing to touch his skin, to drag my nails down his chest and draw blood. To reach inside his chest and grip his heart. I wanted to consume him. All of him. I would not be sated until I had.

Mesmerised, he stared at me in horror and confusion as I leaned down for a kiss. Our lips locked and I held him there, clamping my mouth around his. He struggled beneath me, but still I held firm, drinking his breath into my lungs.

Vairnruth's hands found my shoulders once more, trying to push me off. I heard Louisa shouting my name, a mere echo, as if from a distance. As I swallowed Vainruth's breath, my body spasmed, waves of ecstasy coursing through me. In the moment of weakness that afforded, Louisa was able to pull me back, breaking the seal I had formed against her brother's mouth.

He clutched at his throat, face blue, eyes bulging. I pushed Louisa off me, ignoring the little twinge of guilt I felt as she tumbled to the ground, and turned back to her brother. Vairnruth no longer had the power in him to speak. His chest rose and fell increasingly slowly, every breath a battle. He was drowning on dry land. Triumph rushed to my head.

Vairnruth gripped my arm, his fingernails digging into my scales.

"Ondine. I did ... love you." His dying eyes flashed gold in the sunlight. Was he the Fairie King? Was he just a man, after all? It didn't matter to me anymore. He was unimportant.

"Not the way I wanted."

I bent over him, kissed him once more, long and slow, as he gasped his last useless breath. He fell back against the sand, his face black and withered, already a corpse.

As Vairnruth's lifeless body wasted on the sand, I turned to the rest of the guests. Neither my rage nor my hunger was yet sated. Every nerve in my body screamed for more. There was a moment of pause, a pregnant silence as all around me held their breath, and then I launched myself upon the nearest partygoer.

All was a blur to me. I had no thought or care for who I was hurting—there was only hunger and need, and souls for me to swallow. I pinned the man to the ground, crouching over him, and pressed my mouth to his, feeling a short-lived rush of relief as his life flowed into me. The moment I let him go, I moved on to the next, and the next.

With each victim I became stronger, faster. Plenty ran, but I was quick enough to catch them before they got too far. Before long, the ground around me was strewn with blackening bodies.

But it was not enough. Somewhere in the back of my mind, I knew I could take and take, and it would never be enough.

The next thing I knew, I held Louisa in my arms. She trembled as I stretched my mouth open, ready to swallow her, to make her soul a part of me.

"Emma! Emma!" Her eyes were wide with terror. "Please. This isn't you!"

This is me, I wanted to hiss. *This has always been me.* But I could not speak. I had been trapped in the Moon Lake for too long. Cursed, starved, and abused. Now that I was surrounded by souls, I could only feed.

I lunged for Louisa, but she slipped from my grip and ran. I spun round, intending to follow her, but my movements were slowing. Being out of the water was beginning to harm me. My newly scaled skin was drying, my breath growing shallow and difficult.

Desperate, I pounced on the nearest figure—one of the few remaining—hoping to gain some much-needed strength. I could sense the human's soul flickering as I prepared to devour it.

But wait—not just *one* soul.

Two. Two souls located in one body. It was enough to make me pause. Puzzlement brought me back to my senses a little and I recognised my sister. She stared up at me from the ground, her face contorted in horror, and I realised that the second soul, small but bright, was her baby.

A cacophony of memories flooded my mind, some Ondine's, some my own. Amidst Ondine's hatred and fury for vengeance, scenes of my childhood replayed: Charlotte, helping me learn to read. Charlotte, pushing me on the swing our father had hung on a tree in our garden. Dressed in white at the altar on her wedding day, shining with pride. The glow in her cheeks as she told me she was expecting a child.

Charlotte had never been my enemy. She had only followed her own path, as I had to follow mine.

"Emma, don't!"

Louisa hurried back towards me. Had she simply fled, I could not have followed her—she must have understood that. She must have seen how I was ailing. But instead of escaping, she chose to return. To stop me from killing my sister. From doing something for which I could never forgive myself.

Slowly, I got to my feet, backing away from Charlotte. Her expression of horror reflected the monster I had become, and she wasted no time in hurrying away. But Louisa remained.

"What happened to you, dear Emma?" she asked, her voice little more than a whisper.

"He took me." I walked towards her, water sloshing over the ground with my every step. "He captured me. He brought me here."

Louisa shook her head. "That wasn't you." It hurt to see her back away from me, her hands raised, ready to defend herself if necessary. I didn't want this: I didn't want to be this creature, destroying everything around me without thought or reason. Somewhere in the back of my mind, I sensed that Ondine felt the same, deep beneath the layers of bitterness and resentment she'd built up to protect herself.

"It *was* me." I could speak only with difficulty, but this felt important. I reached out, cupped her face in my hands. "It was all of us."

She looked in my eyes, and I think she understood. She had been as much Vairnruth's prisoner as anybody else. And if it hadn't been her brother, it would have been a husband, a father, an uncle. All women had a jailer. Every last one of us. I took a long, rattling breath.

"You're dying," she whispered.

"I need ... the water. I need to be ... free."

"I'll get you to the lake." Louisa started to drag me back to the water, but I held her fast.

"No ... not the lake ... there's no way out."

I had no breath left to say more. I looked at her pleadingly, willing her to read my mind, see my meaning. I could not go back to that prison. I grasped her hand and tried to do what Ondine had done for me, sending my thoughts and memories to Louisa. At least, some of them were my thoughts and memories. I could no longer figure out where I ended and Ondine began. All at once, I was Emma Crawford, and the water nymph, and the innocent girl who'd swum in the lake and happened to meet the Faerie King. I was every woman who'd ever been imprisoned, restricted, forced to stop thinking for herself, suffocated by the weight of society's rules.

And then I understood.

Louisa was the one. The one who loved me enough to set me free.

20

Louisa helped me out to the stable yard. Desperate for water, I dunked my face in one of the troughs, holding it under as long as I could while Louisa hastily saddled up a horse. When she dragged me away from the trough, I moved with reluctance, almost fighting against her in my desire to get back to the water.

But Louisa was forceful, in a way that surprised me. She helped me onto the horse and hopped up behind me, riding like a man, one arm wrapped around my waist to stop me from falling.

She spurred the animal to a canter, and we rode across the park beyond the Abbey. Past the lake, through the woods. I clung to the horse's mane, paralysed by my need for water. My skin was dry and flaking, my lungs burning. No matter how much air I sucked down, nothing assuaged the tightening of my chest. I was drowning. Letting go of the horse with one hand, I felt around my neck until I found the tell-tale flaps of newly emerged gills. If I didn't get beneath the water soon, I would die.

I twisted in my seat, trying to look up at Louisa, to make

her understand the gravity of my situation, but my throat was so parched I could not speak. Thankfully, she rode fast, her face a picture of grim determination.

"Just hang on," she told me. "It's not far now."

I grew limp, black spots invading my vision. The air was a cage encircling me, squeezing my lungs like a vice. Delirious thoughts swam through my mind, memories of the carnage I had wreaked upon Vairnruth's party. I watched myself as if from above, devouring soul after soul, driven by a terrible hunger that was unrecognisable even to myself. What sort of monster had I become? Perhaps I deserved to die.

Finally we came to a river. Louisa reined in the horse and helped me dismount. I was weak and fainting in her arms, but the moment my feet touched the rushing water I let out a sigh of relief. Without even looking back at my saviour, I threw myself into the water and dove beneath the surface, lingering there a long while as the life rushed back to my body. My strength returned, my scales regained their shine. Utter delight rushed through me as the water sang of its journey from the mountains to the open sea. A vista opened up, promising oceans and faraway shores, adventure and freedom. My heart longed to see every corner of the Earth, to taste every experience.

But first, I had someone to thank.

I surfaced to find Louisa still crouched on the bank. Her worried face lit up with joy when she saw me, and I felt a terrible pang of sadness at the thought that I might never see her again.

"Thank you." I lifted my hand and entwined my now-webbed fingers with her slender, human ones. "You saved my life."

"I still don't understand what happened, dear Emma. Ondine. I don't even know what I should call you now." A little hiccupping laugh escaped her—something close to a sob. "I suppose I was never that clever."

"I came here to find out if there was more to life than the path my father mapped out for me. It turns out there is." I kissed her fingers. "There is the sea, and freedom. And there is you. So much more than I expected or ever imagined." I was silent for a moment, thinking of the terrible harm I had done to Vairnruth and the others. "I'm so sorry, Louisa. For your brother. For everything."

Tears filled Louisa's eyes. "My brother tried to control something he could not understand. That was his error, I suppose. He made a prisoner of you. How could he expect you not to fight back?" From the sad look that crossed her face, I could tell she was thinking of her own long imprisonment, all the time she'd spent lonely and friendless in Northwood Abbey because of her brother's jealousy. "I wish I could come with you."

"You are the lady of Northwood Abbey now." I reminded her. "You need answer to no-one. The world is at your feet."

"And yet all I want is right here." She leaned over and kissed me, one last time. For a moment, I was afraid her touch would awaken my hunger again, but it did not—I trusted her to release me, and she did.

I let myself be caught in the water's flow, diving below and surfacing again in pure joy at its caress on my skin. With one final glance at Louisa's face, I allowed the river to take me. Down the river, out to the sea, and beyond.

To freedom.

ABOUT THE AUTHOR

Antonia Rachel Ward is an author of horror and speculative fiction, based in Cambridgeshire, UK. Her short stories and poetry have been published by Flame Tree Press, the British Science Fiction Association, and Dark Recesses, among others.

She is the author of two novellas, *Marionette* and *Attack of the Killer Tumbleweeds!*, and her first novel, *DreamScape*, was self-published in October 2023. In 2024 her first poetry chapbook, *The Patron*, was published by Querencia Press. Another novel, *Infernal Fruit*, is forthcoming in 2025.

She is also the founder and editor-in-chief of Ghost Orchid Press, and has edited multiple anthologies.